THE MIKVAH QUEEN

THE MIKVAH QUEEN

Jennifer Natalya Fink

悟り

Rebel Satori Press

Bar Harbor, Maine

Published in the United States of America by
REBEL SATORI PRESS
P.O. Box 363
Hulls Cove, ME 04644
www.rebelsatori.com

Book design by Sven Davisson
Cover photo by Sarah Sohn

Library of Congress Cataloging-in-Publication Data

Fink, Jennifer.
   The mikvah queen / Jennifer Natalya Fink.
      p. cm.
   ISBN 978-1-60864-031-7 (pbk.)
   1. Jewish girls--Fiction. 2. Cancer--Patients--Fiction. 3. Neighbors--Fiction.
   4. Mikveh--Fiction. 5. Purity, Ritual--Judaism--Fiction. 6. Ithaca (N.Y.)--Fiction. 7. Jewish fiction. I. Title.
   PS3606.I54M55 2010
   813'.6--dc22
                          2010015090

For the Two Ns-

Nadia Sohn Fink

and

Nancy Ring

PROLOGUE:
SUNDAY NIGHT

So how the hell did the world begin?

Come on, how did it all start? Don't be a dope; you know the answer.

I don't know. Stop bugging me. How come you don't know? Aren't you supposed to know, like, everything?

Okay, okay. You don't have to answer. I'll tell you a joke instead:
It's Friday night at the mikvah. The women are all jostling to be first on line, squabbling like a bunch of ninnies. "Let me go first," says the first one. "I'm the Rebbetzin, the Rebbe's wife, and the Rebbe is waiting for me."
"No, no, let me go first," says the next one. "I'm Moishe the Doctor's wife, and the Doctor is waiting for me."
"No, I should go," says another. "I'm Shlomo the Tailor's wife, and the Tailor is waiting for me."
"No, me," says yet another lady, giving the others a push. "I'm Abe the Peddler's wife, and the Peddler is waiting for me."
Suddenly, a poorly dressed woman pushes her way to the front of the line.
"I must go first," she announces. "I'm Rachel, the prostitute. I'm nobody's wife, but the whole town is waiting for me!"

1

I don't get it. What does that have to do with the creation of the world?

Nothing. Everything. The diet sodas, the mirror balls, and Leah: they all came later. But in the beginning, there was mikvah.

What? I don't get it. Your stupid jokes don't make sense, God. I'm falling back to sleep. Goodnight.

What?! Who the hell gave you the idea that I'm God?

CHAPTER ONE:
MONDAY

Charlene Walkeson

I never liked other people's children. Their greasy hands, those beady eyes, the tendency of their hair to fall in strings around their ears. Oh, I tolerated them well enough when my daughter Mary was small. I'd host the requisite birthday parties; I'd pop popcorn, tell ghost stories, nod my head as they told their long, rambling stories. As I'd listen, I'd try not to focus on the funny smell of their breath, sweet and sweat mingling as they talked on and on. I managed.

Once Mary was grown, I ignored children. I didn't miss them.

When Susie was born and I became a grandmother, I feared it might start all over again: the noisy birthday parties, the gangs of kids tramping through my living room, the expectation that I'd not only allow other peoples' kids to invade my house, but relish the opportunity. The fat-cheeked girls with sweaty palms, their frizzy pig tails held together by elastic bands; boys, the little fidgety boys who couldn't sit down, racing around my dining room table; and worst of all, the pouty pre-teen girls in lipstick and long johns, sulking at some imagined insult during those sleepless slumber parties: I had already suffered through it all. So even when Mary ditched her husband and left Susie here with me, I stuck to my guns. No birthday parties, no sleep-overs, no friends for dinner, I vowed. No more. I will ignore children.

But now, here I am, lying in my cold bed at dawn, looking out my window into the unlit window of the house next door, thinking of Jane.

Jane Schwartz

Barely alive, barely alive, ha ha ha ha barely alive, belts Jane's father from the kitchen. Ever since he got the *Mad* magazine mini-album with thirty minutes of non-stop disco parodies, he's been playing it non-stop each morning. Today he's flipping pancakes to it, forcing the fake disco hits to waft through the house. From her bedroom, Jane cannot make out the words; just the beat and the melody, identical to the original hits from which the silly parodies are derived. Ha ha ha ha barely alive. She can never make out the words on the radio anyway; she habitually fills in obscene lyrics in their absence.

The alarm clock's radio blares on, turn the beat around clashing with Dad and *Mad* in an unrehearsed trio. Disco: yuck. Nobody listens to disco anymore.

She sucks as she listens, covers pulled up to her neck, the wet black tendril lacing its way down her throat. The longer her hair grows, the more she craves it. Not the hair, not the sucking even, but the rush of relief shadowing each individual suck. Her mother doesn't allow Jane to wash

4

her hair more than once a week, convinced that the harsh chemicals in the water interfere with her delicate body chemistry. Jane dowses her hair in the bathroom sink each morning anyway, so that she can come to school with hair dripping from the shower like all the other girls in the sixth grade.

A new song is on the radio now, a country-western ballad Jane doesn't recognize, but Dad is still belting out barely alive, barely alive, holding each note louder and longer than the singers on the record. Jane sucks harder, the hair bundling tight around her tongue like a roughly woven basket. Take that out of your mouth, her mother scolds automatically each morning. The swallowed hair will clump in your stomach, turn to topsoil, sprout plant life if you don't stop sucking. She doesn't stop sucking. She takes one lock at a time tongue wrapped in long black strands microscopic digestive bacteria breaking down remnants of Breck creme rinse. Smooth as a Breck girl she draws the hair out of her mouth with one finger, feeling it play upon her lips. Old food, old hair, suck tight, don't swallow. Glory, glory.

She tightens her throat into a fist, eyes tearing as she resists the urge to spit or swallow. Barely alive, barely alive, he blares, slightly ahead of the record. Spit pours out onto the pillow, her throat clenching tighter turn the beat around covers pulled tight around her ha ha ha turn it upside down covering face mouth hair. She imagines being underwater. The oxygen disappears with each passing second. The weight of the water pushes her to the bottom of the ocean, while fish, tiny silver fish, swim beneath her arms, circling in silent schools through her hair. Today is Monday.

Today is a sick day, she decides, lumbering waterlogged

5

into the kitchen. No school today.

Barely alive, barely alive, he flips the pancakes high as he sings, stooping over the stove in his underwear, balls bulging out at the sides like internal organs which accidentally popped out. Kidneys, or pancreases, except you only have one pancreas.

"Have you been sucking your hair again, Jane? It's all dry and frizzy."

She doesn't answer.

"How am I supposed to braid it for you when you've already sucked the life out of it?" He is putting too much butter in the pancake pan, determined not to allow the batter to stick to the bottom. Smoke wisps up from the pan.

"I'm not going to school. I'm sick. My head hurts, and I threw up." Vomit nauseates him: she knows he will not ask for details. Lying on the spot is her specialty.

"Well, Mom is already at school, and I have meetings at the lab all day."

"Well, I'm sick," she says, trying her best to look mournful.

"If you're really too sick for school, you know you'll have to go next door to Mrs. Walkeson. Are you too sick for pancakes?"

The burnt butter smell really is making her nauseous now. "Yeah."

Back in bed, Jane fakes sleep until she hears him crack the door open and whisper 'good-bye.' She waits under the covers, until she hears the car screech as it hurries out of the driveway, then waits an extra moment.

The silence of the house at ten a.m. She listens for the buzz of the refrigerator, only audible when the house is absolutely empty. Hear oh Israel the Lord is God the Lord is One.

6

Shmah Y'Israel Adonai Elohanu Adonai Ehad. Everything hums together, a woodpecker outside, the refrigerator, her own breathing. Everything buzzing as one.

The smooth hum of the house pulls her back to the dream, to the voice: *How did the world begin? And how the hell did mikvah begin?*

Who would ask such retarded questions? As she throws the covers off the bed and strips out of her Snoopy nightshirt, Jane tries to remember exactly what the voice sounded like. She stops up her ears with her fingers, blocking out the babble of the refrigerator, shmah, woodpecker until she can hear it again.

Come on, how did it all start? The voice is joking and casual, but with an angry undercurrent. Not male, no, not quite, but deep, so deep it's almost a monotone, no tone, a dark thick silence. If it were a color, it would be an overripe plum, verging on prune.

Don't be a dope; you know the answer. Whose voice is it, or was it? Mike's? No, his is smoother, less grating. Definitely not Mike's.

But what about mikvah? You still haven't explained how we got that, missy. You —

"Shut up!" Jane yells out loud. The sound of her own shout startles the voice away. I know who it is, she realizes all at once. I know whose voice this is. It's Mrs. Walkeson's: but Mrs. Walkeson's voice slowed down, deepened, like when you play a record at the wrong speed. What's she doing in my dreams?

"Shut up, shut up!" Jane yells again. If I just don't think about it, it will stay away, she thinks to herself. What should I wear?

7

Jane dresses without washing, choosing a red leotard with red pants and a red leather belt. Not her favorite color, but it feels like a red day today. Red tongue, red eyes, red clothes. She checks the pink underwear she wore to bed last night to see if there are any spots, any signs that it might finally have come, before she changes into fresh red cotton panties. Nothing. Will it be like peeing blood? Will it make her faint to see it, like when the doctor pricks her finger to run a blood test? How much will she bleed? She worries the red cloth between her fingers, pursing her lips. White underwear would be better: easier to spot. But red is all she has clean today. She'd better check and make sure red is kosher. Perhaps there's even a law, a particular edict concerning the proper sort of underwear to make it show better. Rabbi Loewe will know.

Sprawling out on her pink bedspread, she thumbs through the book she's been reading in secret every night for a week: *The Jewish Path in Sex, Love, and Marriage*. The cover is faded, a dark formal blue. Rabbi Maurice Loewe, the author, is a renowned Orthodox rabbi, she reads in the preface, as she gnaws on her hair. Mikvah is his special area of expertise. Rabbi Loewe the mikvah king, expert in all things relating to "family purity," t'annit niddeh. She examines the front pages and then the back pages, careful to turn one page at a time. No, there's no photo. But she's sure she knows what he looks like: a grandfatherly guy, with a long beard and sideburns, a somber cast to his dark, baggy eyes. A real rebbe, properly certified, deep-voiced, old. Not like Mike.

He's not even a real rabbi, Jane's mother always tells her as she drives her twice a week on the forty-five minute trek to Mike's for Talmudic study. He's just some "born-again"

Jew, some grad student who decided Jewish law was cooler than Kant. A freak, a fraud, full of a yenta's half-baked Jewish mishegas mixed with that hippie shit, her father grumbles in the car on the drive back through the dark roads leading out of Ithaca, out toward the wilds of Brooktondale, Slaterville Springs, Caroline, swerving to avoid the hordes of deer that gather at the sharp turn off Ellis Hollow Road to Ellis Highlands on spring nights. She doesn't answer, tightening her metal seat belt buckle around her waist, sucking her hair quietly as he repeats himself, yenta mishegas and hippie shit.

She feels a little guilty now, turning to Rabbi Loewe, like she's betraying Mike just by reading the book, proving her parents right, not believing in the New Jew. "The New Jew needs new rules, a direct line to God," Mike says. Will the New Jew be ready for the mikvah? Lying on her stomach on her bed, she turns to page three, and reads. WHY MIKVAH? Rabbi Loewe asks in bold, underlined letters. And answers:

It's about water. Water from within the body contaminates. Nocturnal emissions, menstrual blood, placenta. Mikvah exists to purify internal waters. "Before the destruction of the second temple in 70 A.D., men would go to the mikvah ("ritual baths") after every nocturnal emission, before their wedding night, and after intercourse." Now women must go, married woman. Starting from the day before their wedding until menopause stills their blood, each Jewish woman must enter the waters of the mikvah and cleanse the microscopic impurities left by her monthly water. Seven days must pass since the last sign of her period is gone before she may enter the mikvah. Seven: Jane's favorite number. Each month, seven lonely days where no man may touch her. Seven days where any object she touches he must avoid, lest he be

9

contaminated. Seven days without sex or touch or mikvah.

Jane looks up "Mikvah—Male" in the back of the book. Only three short entrees. "Originally designed for both sexes, today the mikvah is primarily used as a ritual bath for women, except for a few exceptions, such as conversions. For exceptions, see also conversions: male." The book says nothing about why men no longer go to the mikvah or if women used the mikvah differently in the days of the temple. It doesn't tell how they know why and how frequently men went to the Mikvah before the destruction of the second temple. Why the destruction of the second temple in 70 A.D. destroyed the tradition of male mikvah. Whether there were any men who particularly enjoyed the mikvah, lounging around long after they were cleansed.

It is women, married menstruating women, who must go to the mikvah each month precisely seven days after all traces of their periods have vanished. Only after the mikvah may they resume sexual relations with their husbands. From the moment their period starts until the moment they are purified by the mikvah, they are rendered unclean, contaminating every object around them with just the brush of a finger. Jane runs her fingers against the lampshade beside her bed, over the books piled up on her nightstand, on top of the chair by her desk. Beware the mighty mikvah queen, master of the universe, her Midas touch brings the world to its knees. Only the mikvah waters can save you now! she tells her tomcat Rascal as she throws him off the bed.

She pages through the book some more, unsure of what exactly she's looking for now. Water from outside the body purifies. Two molecules of hydrogen bond steadfastly to a sole ion of oxygen. Two sources of water must be used in the

10

mikvah: running and still. Usually, this amounts to rainwater, collected in a complicated system of pipes and drains, and tap water. Before the mikvah you must wash thoroughly, removing all jewelry, hangnails, Band-Aids, makeup. Rabbinic advice should be sought for temporary fillings, root-canal work or capping in progress, nits in the hair, stitches, casts, unremovable scabs, unusual skin eruptions. You must be pure, you must be free of unsightly nicks and cuts and dirt before you enter the mikvah. Most of all, you must be free of blood. Then you dunk three times, going all the way under, performing the blessing of total immersion. The mikvah attendant cries out "Kosher!" each time you bob to the surface. You are purified, ready for sex.

Kosher! The first mikvah is on your wedding night, the whole wedding planned to coincide with the end of your menstrual cycle. The last is after your last period. What happens if you're irregular? Do you postpone the wedding? Cancel the caterer, photographer, flower girls, mother-in-law? Jane's own mother is blissfully ignorant of mikvah, family purity, purity in general. Jane has asked a few leading questions, which her mother dismissed with "Oh, that's just something they did in the old days, in Europe. I don't think even the Orthodox bother with that mishegas now." But Rabbi Loewe suggests otherwise. "Mikvah is the basis of family purity," he suggests. "Only the woman, the wife, the mother of the family can maintain her family's good sexual and emotional health."

Kosher! A woman must check herself religiously each day after her period seems to be over to check for any remnants. The slightest discoloration renders her impure. There are pages upon pages of Mishnah, commentary heaped upon

11

commentary by the rabbis about the many shapes, sizes, and colors a contaminating splotch can take, each old man tugging excitedly on his beard as he writes one more line about the really foolproof way for a woman to check to make absolutely certain she's truly clean. Use a newly bleached cloth, white and spotless. Use another cloth, and another. But only the woman herself can decide when she is ready for mikvah.

Kosher! Jane sneaks into her mother's office, the former sewing room with the unused sewing machine. Piled on the sewing table are the blue examination books her mother uses to test college freshmen on their knowledge of the Spanish inquisition, thick blue stacks of them. Professor Schwartz, History 237: each booklet in the pile is already labeled in thin red ink, already waiting for the inquisition to fill its blue-lined pages. Jane takes the top one.

Back to her room, lies on her stomach and crosses out History 237 and writes in big black letters:

MIKVAH.

She always puts periods at the end of headings, even though she knows you're not supposed to. And at the end of her name, which she writes carefully below the title. Opening Rabbi Loewe, she finds the how-to section: how to know if you are mikvah-ready. Four easy rules, which fit easily on the first page of the blue test book.

A. Five colors of blood are unclean in a woman.

B. Red, and black, and bright crocus color, and blood like water mixed with earth, and blood like water mixed

with wine.
    C. Water from within the body contaminates.
    D. Water from outside the body purifies.

Five colors of blood are unclean in a woman.
    Not four, or seven, she imagines Mike joking with a half-smile. Five. She hates numbers. What is five? Five fingers, five colors: only "five" links them, blurs them together. She hates blurring.

    Red, and black, and bright crocus color, and blood like water mixed with earth, and blood like water mixed with wine.
    She writes them out individually:

Red
Black
Bright crocus color
Blood like water mixed with earth
Blood like water mixed with wine

    What color are crocuses? She envisions a bouquet of flowers in pink, red, magenta, purple, green, violet, the colors dripping and staining. The colors spill out of the separate petals, flooding the bouquet.
    From the time she could distinguish her vagina from her asshole, Jane feared the bath water would flood her. Enter and never leave, cause drowning or explosion. She knows the cruel laws of molecules. How heat rises. How water rushes to fill a gaping vacuum, how cold falls like frozen lead to

13

the bottom. Or does cold collect at the center? Get stuck as it falls, suspended like a lump in the throat?

Water from within the body contaminates.
Rabbi Loewe elaborates: semen, mucus, vomit. Nocturnal emissions, menstrual blood, placenta.

In the days before the second temple was destroyed, would men gather each morning, crowding the mikvah to dissolve the night's yield of dried semen? She can see them in their skullcaps and Speedos, a pack of dark hairy men in sandals. The water would grow thick with it. Like the Dead Sea, so salty a grown man could float in it.

Water from outside the body purifies.
Another bit of lore from Rabbi Loewe: before you leave the mikvah and re-enter the cold, polluted world, it is a blessing to touch another woman. You talk to no one, not even the mikvah attendant who sees you dunk naked into the mikvah, but you should touch another woman before you leave the baths. Do you brush against her shoulder, clasp her hand, caress her arm? The book does not specify where you should touch her, just that you should touch.

Down's syndrome, slow learners, near-sightedness, hyperactivity, thin hair, attention deficit disorder, cancer. Lack of respect for one's elders. Insincerity. Tay Sach's disease, food allergies, manic depression, bad breath. Crone's disease, athlete's foot, disloyalty to the faith, depression, poor motor skills. These weaknesses of health and character in the child, Jane reads, can all be traced back to a failure of the mother to attend to the laws of mikvah and maintain family purity before, during, and after pregnancy.

In the mirror Jane assesses her thick eyebrows, the mole over her right eye, her slightly yellow complexion. Which of these defects could have been prevented if only her mother had visited the mikvah? She looks sideways, sees the shadow of another Jane, more perfectly formed, more polite to her elders. A taller girl, her skin glows in the light.

During the Holocaust the Nazis closed the mikvahs, Rabbi Loewe reports. The Nazis decried the mikvah as dirty, disease-ridden, even linking mikvah to the imaginary murder of Christian children for use in imaginary Jewish rituals. Locked shut by the Gestapo, left to mold, the mikvahs were abandoned. But the Jewish woman did not despair! Ever-resourceful, determined to maintain her family's purity for the sake of her future children's good health, the Jewish woman built make-shift mikvah in basements, on the trains, even in the camps, careful to make sure that it had the requisite two sources of water. If these Holocaust heroines, true daughters of Sarah, Rebecca, Leah, and Ruth could maintain mikvah under such adverse conditions, surely, surely, Rabbi Loewe implores, today's modern American housewife can bother to go to her local mikvah for the health of her people! It's like a posh spa, really, Rabbi Loewe suggests, a tone of desperation creeping in.

Jane pauses, unable to read further. Those queer old names: Sarah, Rebecca, Leah, Ruth. Shoshanna, Shulamith, Yona. Tears well up and she bites her lip. Jane. Plain Jane, plain Protestant Jane. She will need a better name to make her mikvah. Chavah? Yona? No: Leah.

Ugly Leah. The homely older daughter, slipped in place of Rachel into Jacob's bed. Jacob worked seven years to

15

win the delicate hand of Rachel and instead got the paw of ugly old Leah. It was a classic case: the old bait-and-switch routine, Rabbi Mike tells her. Laban, Leah and Rachel's dad, had watched the way Jacob always favored Rachel, chatting with her in the fields, trying to make her laugh by mimicking Laban's slight lisp, Jacob's hands casually brushing against her thick curls as they talked. He had watched as Leah looked on from the sidelines, pulling her thin straight hair between her fingers, blushing profusely on those rare occasions when Jacob would talk to her, usually only to ask her for some water from the well. But lisping old Laban had the last laugh, leading Leah into Jacob's bed on the night of Jacob and Rachel's wedding. What did Leah think as she waited for him? As he cried out Rachel's name, buried deep inside Leah's body, what was the expression that passed across Leah's face? As Jacob made love to the idea of Rachel, what did Leah think?

Yesterday, Sunday, in the gloom of a late March Ithaca afternoon, slouching in the big burgundy leather chair facing Rabbi Mike's desk, Jane puzzled over Leah and Rachel. She couldn't answer Mike, her mouth filling with strands of hair instead of words. He had stared at her a moment, letting the question hang like thick incense in the air.

He never would answer his own questions. If she didn't offer at least a word, a stray thought, he'd pause, wait, sometimes repeat the question, restate it before moving to another idea. We will come back to this, he says when she doesn't venture an answer. We will come back. And so they had moved on yesterday, to mikvah laws, the t'annit niddeh.

Now, staring in the mirror on this cold Monday morning, widening her eyes to zombie proportions, Jane tries to figure out the answer. What did Leah think? rejected for the beautiful Rachel? unloved, abandoned? Jane flips through her pocket Hebrew Bible, propping it open on the marbleized Formica counter beside the sink. Let's see: The Story of Leah. She reads the story again, looking for clues to Leah.

"When morning came, there was Leah," the Bible states. Ah! Leah did get her revenge after the wedding. After the big switcheroo, when he discovered the trick, found Leah in bed with him where Rachel should have been, Jacob agreed to take both sisters as his wife. So Leah and Rachel were both Jacob's wives, Rachel adored, Leah neglected. Leah alone. "God saw that Leah was neglected, so he opened her womb, while Rachel remained barren." Jane tries to erase the image of an open womb from her mind's eye, a swollen red thing, like a turkey gizzard.

Open wombs: "here's the mikvah connection," she says aloud to her image in the mirror, pretending Mike is listening. Open wombs, reproduction, menstruation: this is all mikvah territory. I get it: you're assigning the story of Leah and the laws of family purity together, because the story of Leah shows what happens when there are no rules and people's wombs just open and close and stuff. She flips open Rabbi Loewe again, and reads the preface:

The modern mikvah is like a spa compared to the dumps our grandmothers in Poland, Russia, Germany, God rest their souls, were forced to use. Surely any modern Jewish woman in her mink fur and two cars can take the hour a month to perform a proper mikvah.

Like a spa. Right next door, down in Mrs. Walkeson's basement is the beginning of a spa: a porta-sauna, a freestanding unit ordered by mail, assembled at home. Jane has overheard Mr. Walkeson promise Mrs. Walkeson that this sauna is just the first step to converting the basement into a complete home spa. It stands alone in a corner now, like a coat closet waiting to be filled. Sometimes on the weekends Jane and Susie sentence their Barbies to the sauna, wait for the gas to pour out of the vents, shave Barbie to her roots, leaving her naked and dying in the sauna as Jane plots her escape.

But this is much bigger than Barbie crematoria. The Walkeson's basement sauna would make a great mikvah, Jane decides.

Charlene

Too near the heat, and the fibers melt. Wigs are delicate creatures. They turn so easily from flaxen curls to lumpy plastic. Even a hot lamp can spoil the fibers. Like turned milk, they smell a bit off at first. Then the blondes gum up into plastic slime, the redheads turn orange, the brunettes ash.

Monday morning, six a.m., and the house is sleeping. Dusty dry heat spews from noiseless vents. I can taste it in the air: a burned flavor, stale, as if warm summer air had been canned for months and lost all freshness. Today only the bathtub, its white porcelain sides gleaming in the light, can offer relief from this heat. In the empty tub I lie myself down, turn on the water, and wait for it to cover me.

I lie back in the tub, my head floating up, a white balloon

bobbing on the sea. Water runs to bone. Breaks down fat and gristle, muscle and grey matter, liver and pancreas. Reduce me back to hydrogen and oxygen, water and air, I pray silently. Break me down to gold fillings, prime numbers, polished bones. Dissolve me.

After one bath ends I crave another. Sometimes I haven't even dried off from the first bath before I begin the second. The tub still half-full, my arms dripping onto the gold rug, I turn back before I've even left the bathroom, back to the tub, its white porcelain bed.

Afterwards, I let my bare feet drip on the gold rug, disregarding my own admonitions about mold and athlete's foot, and get to work on my toenails. When I was a child, my mother would pedicure my feet. I would sit on the kitchen chair, my mother kneeling at my feet, separating each toe from the others with soft white cotton balls. The pedicure kit was pink plastic, filled with steel instruments resembling a surgeon's tools. I'd pretend that she was the doctor, with an invisible nurse handing her the instruments. Knife? knife. Scalpel? scalpel. I would gaze at the back of her blond head bent beneath mine as she scraped the dirt out from under each nail, digging into the flesh with a pointy, sharp instrument. I'd watch her bun come undone as she pushed back my cuticles with her fingers. I loved to watch her hair unravel. Cuticles trimmed, nails cut and filed, Pond's cream massaged into my arches, I would reign on my kitchen throne, staring down at her raw fingers rubbing away the remains of my calluses.

She'd finish off with a bit of homemade peppermint lotion, mineral oil mixed with a few drops of peppermint extract. The smell would waft up to my face all day. Afterwards, she

19

was ragged from her efforts, brow sweating, hair undone. I would sit barefoot for a while after the pedicure, admiring my toes. For the rest of the day, my feet would look like two soft candies, pink and pliable.

Is it too late to start such regal treatment in my own house now? Perhaps my Susie would permit me to give her a pedicure, if I could convince her that Barbie and Midge liked them.

My own daughter doesn't like for me to touch her much now. When she was a baby, it was a different story. Nothing brought a giggle to my daughter's face when she was on the brink of tears like a little lotion rubbed on her butt or tummy. I'd use a dab of pink lotion, scented with that too-sweet artificial baby shit smell. She'd giggle and coo, gazing up at me as if the lotion were the punch line of a magnificent private joke. But once she started grade school, she'd cringe with disgust whenever I try to give her more than a quick peck on the cheek. I doubt she even remembers our pedicures anymore. With Susie, I am hesitant to ask, afraid that she will give me that too-polite, slightly condescending smile and say, "No thank you, Grandma," and wriggle away.

The water dripping from my feet has turned the gold rug an ugly shade of hot-dog mustard brown. I dry my feet off with a hand-towel, and face the mirror. My bones ache, and a terrible tightness seizes my chest. Today must unfold, the day must be filled. I ignore the army of pills awaiting me in the cabinet. Maybe that Jane girl next door, plain Jane with her frizzing curls and wild eyes, would like a pedicure. Perhaps she would allow such fawning. She loves anything with lots of steps, intricate procedures, rules, more rules.

Jane Schwartz, with her hair sucking and Hebrew. A

smarter girl than Susie, and more fragile somehow. She'd make a great policy analyst, one of those women with big glasses and expensive suits who rattles off long chains of figures without blinking. Or a lawyer, a smart Jewish lawyer, maybe, talking fast and funny, with bright red lipstick.

In Washington we had lots of Jews. Surrounding every blonde big-jawed candidate were a dozen nimble Jews, trailing after him like a pack of worried ghosts. With their cold cut lunches eaten in the office, their ability to work later and harder than the rest of us, and their rapid-fire jokes, they quickly became a prized item, a feature no decently run department could afford to be without. They came in the '50s, first in a gray-flannelled Eisenhower trickle, then clean-cut Kennedy Dems with boundless enthusiasm. Even that moron Ford brought a few, gray Jews with potbellies and shrill wives. My last year in Washington, Carter and his born-again cadres rolled in with a gang of Jews to forecast the economic weather, tell the bad news, massage the numbers. I loved those guys, even learned to love their loud quick jokes, the spicy aroma of their thick pastrami sandwiches that lingered into the next day's coffee.

In the Commerce Department we had as many as we could find. "It's Feingold, Feinstein, or Fineberg," Bill would joke whenever one called me at home, "I can't keep those damn kike names straight."

"Fineman. His name is Fine*man*," I'd say in exasperation, cupping the mouthpiece so Joe Fineman wouldn't have to hear. Joe was the kind about whom everyone secretly says, "He doesn't look Jewish," not Joe, with his straight nose and thin blonde hair.

It's hard to imagine Fineman with these new Reagan

spooks. He's still in the loop, left there with the leftovers, the dumbest of the Nixon bunch, plus these new little boys fresh out of college, full of Jesus and job cuts and Christ knows what other idiotic schemes for destroying the economy. "They won't listen to me. To the facts, the numbers. They pay me to analyze data, write reports, make predictions, and then they smile that shit-eating Jesus freak smile, 'Thank you, Mr. Fineman,' and never even open the goddamn report," Fineman bitched to me on the phone last week. Even Nixon knew enough to listen to Fineman.

Feingold. Feinstein. Fineberg. I mouth the words into the mirror. "We always knew you were an egghead," Fineman might joke if he saw me now. Only a Jew would be able to crack a joke about chemo.

When we moved out here two years ago, the last thing I thought I'd miss would be Fineman's sarcasm, tangy as hot pastrami. I was looking forward to my early retirement, a new job for Bill at the local branch of Borg-Warner, a new house, a new doctor. And relaxation, lots of it, doctor's orders. I don't miss the job itself; thirty years of being a government accountant was quite enough, thank you. But I miss the Jews.

Oh, I suppose there are a few out here, young professors with their economy cars and solar houses. They are so serious, so confident; only their noses and curls set them apart from the other professors. And of course there are the hippies, those aging Cornell dropouts and recent Ithaca College grads who populate every public park. Even the hippie Jews are industrious, opening yet another head shop or organic co-op or Indian dress-and-rug palace downtown. But no Finemans, no sharp tongues to mock my bald head.

I sit on the edge of the tube, resisting the urge to start

another bath, and massage some cream into my feet. My toes look small, unhappy to be stuck there at the end of my large feet. What would Jane Schwartz's mother think of my pedicures? I can picture her giving me that tight-lipped smile. Despite their passive solar house and university jobs, the Schwartzs don't really seem Jewish. They're just more efficient, slightly brighter versions of the WASPS who've moved out here to take advantage of the cheap real estate and clean air. Like Bill and me.

An out-of-date auburn wig, a '60s mod number with big bangs that curl under when it rains, lies in the corner near the towel rack. A leftover from the Inauguration, for Kennedy, my first one. You needed a good wig to make it with the Camelot crowd.

I grab it, popping it on my head without bothering to brush it. Jane, on the other hand, seems all Jew to me. Jane Schwartz, queen of Israel, her frizzy hair set in luxurious curls cascading down her neck, a crimson dress snaking down her skinny body. When she grows up, she will be a great beauty, with strong features and a mane of auburn curls. Or maybe she'll remain a plain mousy Jane. It's hard to tell which. Susie, on the other hand, is an easy bet: she'll be a prom-queen beauty who peaks at eighteen and then quickly fades, aging too fast from all that sun and soda pop. But Jane could be a real Jane Russell. All she would need to add would be a slight smirk at the corner of her full lips, and she'd be a head-turner, heart breaker. If she'd just stop chewing her damn hair!

We'll have a pedicure, I resolve, next time Jane stops by. A proper pedicure, with all the pink lotion and fancy equipment I can find.

CHAPTER TWO:
TUESDAY

Jane

So Leah, how did we get blood? Huh?

Well, it all started after God made that first Adam.

Soon, there were many Adams. Only Adams, no Eves. Just a bunch of Adams, running around buck-naked, building tree houses and breaking out in chicken-fights.

Everyone was happy, except God. Sick of singing "I Feel Love," He swam to the shore, and walked to where the Adams were gathered on land, hoping some of the Adams would feel like hanging out with Him. But they were all too busy building tree forts and having chicken-fights to even notice stinky old God.

However, one of the Adams stood apart from the rest. This Adam was a particularly puny one, only five feet tall or so, and his nose was bleeding like crazy. Adam sat on the shore, watching the ocean's tides come in and out while the others built, bleeding and crying. He had terrible posture. "You'll get a back-ache, hunching over like that," God thought as He watched him. Adam's nose bled down his neck, onto his chest. Mucus and blood spilled out of his nose, clinging to the hairs surrounding his nipples.

God sniffed the air as He watched. A new smell: hair

grease, gasoline, ethanol, blood, and something God couldn't quite place. God knew exactly where the smell was coming from, but was too polite to say anything to Adam about it. Besides, Adam was ignoring God. All Adam did was bleed from his nose, let the blood catch on his nipple-hairs, and stare at the ocean. The ocean ran up to his toes, but never touched him.

"Why doesn't Adam just wash off in the damn water?" God thought to Himself, but He was brought up not to say such things in public. The air stank with Adam's nosebleed.

Four days passed. Adam's nose was bleeding even harder now, the two nipples were covered with the stuff, and the whole globe reeked. God just couldn't take the smell anymore. He strode over to Adam, puffed out His chest to look all scary and tough, and yelled, "Adam, would you give it a rest? You've been bleeding for a month. It's starting to really stink around here. Could you, like, wash off in the ocean, at least?"

Adam ignored Him. He didn't even acknowledge that God had spoken; he just kept bleeding onto his nipples and staring out at the ocean. If I pretend it's not happening, Adam thought, it'll go away. God will get off my back, the bleeding will stop, and everything will go back to normal. Maybe I'll even build forts with the other Adams.

But it didn't stop. In fact, it got worse. "Adam, this is really a problem. I can't take the smell anymore. If you don't do something about your, er, nose issue, I'll have to, I don't know," God fished for an appropriate threat. There were no rules, and no punishments, so God wasn't quite sure what to do. Then it came to Him. "I'll have to curse you!" God was excited by the thought: a curse, yeah, that'd be cool.

25

Adam kept bleeding, and kept ignoring Him, keeping his gaze fixed on the ocean. This is not happening, Adam told himself.

Hmm, what kind of curse should I make up? I could put some flimsy paper wings on him, and turn him into that ugly girl with the horsy face who always has to be the smart one on *Charlie's Angels*, God thought. Or I could put him in a dress and throw him down to hell, where all the other naughty Adams would beat the shit out of him for being such a damn sissy. Nah. Too easy. I've got it! God was excited now. He had the perfect curse.

So God, in His deepest, loudest God-voice, cursed: "You think bleeding is so great? Okay, I'll let you bleed. But not from your nose. From your crotch, for four days out of every thirty. And that's not all. No siree! I freeze you here, with your nipples mounded up with mucus and blood and God knows what other crap. No matter how much you wash, you'll have two mounds sitting on your chest, until you die." And in a huff, God marched back into the ocean, never to return.

The other Adams suddenly noticed Adam bleeding. "Gross!" cried the leader of the pack, pointing to the blood trickling from between Adam's legs. "Look, the sissy is bleeding down there! Eeeewwe!!" The other Adams thought this was Adam's name: Ewe. But God, that old codger, misheard the ewwee as Eve. And so he was called Eve, from that moment forth.

"What the hell is wrong with you, Eve?" the Adams asked, but she just kept bleeding, still staring at the ocean, refusing to tell about the nosebleed. This isn't happening, she thought, ignoring the Adams, ignoring God. If I just stand still and don't respond to them, it'll go away and eventually

I'll be an Adam again. But she kept on bleeding from her crotch, the mounds on her chest grew into two fleshy breasts, and the hair congealed to cover it all up. And there were lots of rules, to make sure it stayed all covered.

Okay, I'll buy that bit about the blood. But that doesn't explain the mikvah.

I'm getting to that.

Do you know the way to Santa Fe?

What?!

Do you know the way to Santa Fe? I'll blah blah blah blah, dooby dooby...

As her eyes open, Jane sees her father at the foot of her bed, singing along with her clock-radio, *I know the way to Santa Fe*, dancing to the music in a herky-jerky version of the Hustle. Holding a spatula, he points up to the right, down to the left. In his other hand, he carries a jug of maple syrup with a fat black lady in some kind of turban smiling out on the label. "Do you know the way to French toast-a-fe? French toast is only for the healthy," he sings, turning down the clock radio and humming the way to Santa Fe all the way back to the kitchen.

I'm not going to school, she thinks as she pulls off the covers and pulls on an old, raggedy plaid bathrobe of green, red, and black. I'm wearing all red today and I'm starting a shul with Mrs. Walkeson. Or maybe I'll just build a mikvah. Or maybe I'll throw up.

She puts on a pair of flip-flops, plastic yellow flip-flop sandals designed for sandy beaches and aquamarine swimming pools that she's been using as slippers around the house all winter. Or maybe I'll just stay in bed in my flip-flops. But no school, she decides. Absolutely no school. Shul, not school. She rolls the word around on her tongue. Shul shul shul.

I want to make a shul, she thinks clearly, as the clock-radio blasts on again, this time a high-pitched series of buzzes blaring instead of the radio and Santa Fe. She crawls back under the covers and clenches her eyes and rubs and thinks shul shul shul.

After all, before Jane knew about mikvah, before she really understood what it was, she wanted shul. From the beginning, way back in fifth grade, when her parents first sent her off every Sunday "So you can make your own informed decision," as her mother said, never specifying what it was she was supposed to make an informed decision about, Jane loved shul.

She refused to call it "Sunday school," resolutely ignored how the air of the Ithaca Progressive Jewish Union was suffused with the delicious scent of bacon frying. Even though the Jewish Union held its classes in small meeting rooms in the balcony of the Cornell University Student Center on Sundays, despite the fact that the teachers were mostly ex-hippies who had just themselves rediscovered the coolness of Judaism, its mystical rituals and wailing music, regardless of the bacon frying up for student lunches below, Jane insisted that this was *shul*, and that Mike Silverstein, the self-appointed director of the whole enterprise, be called *Rebbe*. At dinner on Sunday nights she would correct her parents if they slipped, if they dared ask how Sunday school was, or what nonsense Mike was pumping into her head. "He's a *rebbe* and it's a *shul*," she'd interrupt.

From the start, Jane demanded to be placed in the class with the older kids because the guy who did real Talmud and modern Hebrew, Mike someone with thick black sideburns not a rabbi but a true rebbe teacher, Ph.D. in maybe Yiddish, Mike did older kids only.

Eventually, Mike took her on as a private student, a privilege granted only the smartest kids. We're resurrecting an ancient practice, Talmudic pairing, in which a teacher and a student learn by reading together, every day, four eyes glued as one to the page, he told her when he first asked her to consider one-on-one Torah study twice weekly, on Sundays and Wednesdays, to be held in his house. You'll read at home, then read with me, a small Torah portion, along with all the rebbes' commentaries, every week. Side by side. In Hebrew and English. Like a boy in a Warsaw shul would study before the war. It's serious stuff, not this pre-Bat Mitzvah, add a little mishnah and stir, instant Jew crap. Can you handle it?

She stopped going to the group classes, since it was too much driving for her parents to tolerate, and instead went twice a week to Mike's house, Wednesday and Sunday afternoons, for three-hour sessions of close Talmudic study.

"This is the real thing, Jane," he said the first time they met alone in his dark study, eyes burning into her, marking her pale brown stare with their charcoal black. "Only a few kids can really hack it: all the Hebrew, the endless laws, the crazy quilt of commentaries radiating out from the central text on each page. Can you handle it?" Her father hates all the driving, but as her mother says, "Hey, David, two shots of hippie Jewdom a week should inoculate her against Christmas trees and local boys with bad teeth and snowmobiles."

Her father grumbles, "I can't believe I'm allowing my

own daughter to learn all this mishegenah Jewish nonsense; the next thing you know she'll be demanding we buy separate dishes for milk and meat and all that other crap: candle lighting on Fridays, no driving on Shabbos, no lobster even, the whole crazy megillah." But each session, they just talk. Mike and Jane, side-by-side, reading a page of Torah together, or debating the law, sitting directly across from each other.

Now she's in the big time, the private pre-Bat Mitzvah three-time-a-week only-for-the-serious sessions. Can you handle it?

Each week begins with a series of questions. "So what does this week's portion tell us?" Before her coat was off, before he led her to the little windowless study between the bedroom with the ancient lace coverlet and the white bathroom, before she dissected the portion or learned some bit of ritual or history or Hebrew, they would talk. And sweat.

Even in the subzero chill factor upstate winters, Mike Silverstein always seemed to be sweating. Sweat and talk: the words pushed moisture through his black hair, soaking through his yarmulke, his mustache. Jane had never seen a mustache as black and thick as his. They started at four on Sundays and Wednesdays and talked Torah until one of her parents remembered to pick her up around seven. Sitting in the car on the long, hilly ride home, she'd find her own clothes soaked through, clammy against her skin. In the beginning there was shul. And sweat.

As she rolls around under the covers, rubs the soft cloth belt of the old plaid bathrobe between her legs, rubs out of time to the even, loud electronic blasts of the clock- radio, the flip-flops wet with sweat, slipping off her bare feet. She tosses herself out of bed, strips off the bathrobe, and decides: I will wear all red today. I will make my own private shul. She imagines a great big brick shul, with Rabbi Loewe leading her and Mike in secret prayers. The sweat is cooling now, drying on her legs, arms, thighs. Ugh.

Who wants a stinky old shul, anyway? It's no better than regular school, really. Regular school, full of loud kids and math problems and games of soccer. Double ugh. School, Caroline Elementary, full of ugly metal desks, loud soccer games, and the smell of lemony disinfectant. I'm not going to school and I'm not making a shul, Jane decides.

Instead of getting ready for school, she picks at a scab on her arm and sucks a piece of overgrown hair, an ex-bang that her mother hasn't made her trim yet. Jane hates getting her hair cut. Hates anyone touching her hair, arranging it. She likes it like this: uncombed, damp, frizzing up in her mouth. She pulls another piece of bang in and sucks hard, her mouth alive with the hairy taste of it.

The image of the brick shul fades. Instead, she imagines her neighbor, Mrs. Walkeson, a huge curly red wig on her head, up to her neck in water. She doesn't look sick anymore. Mrs. Walkeson, smiling out of a big bathtub. A mikvah, built inside the empty, dry portable sauna sequestered away inside the dank cluttered world of the Walkeson's basement. A mikvah would be even better than a shul. Cleaner, less sweaty. Yes, they should definitely make a mikvah instead of a shul.

Jane pulls the hair out of her mouth and sits up in the bed. "Dad," she calls out. "I'm sick again. I just threw up again. I'm staying home today."

31

Charlene

When my daughter Mary was born, I would shift the position of her skull every four hours to mold her head into a perfect sphere. I smoothed her flesh like a potter uneasy at the wheel, shaping her head beneath my cautious palms. Right up until she entered junior high I would check the shape now and then, trying to feel beneath the barrettes to see if the perfect globe was still unmarred. By the time Sam was born, I no longer had time for such fussing; molding perfect heads went the way of boiled pacifiers. And now with Susie? Forget it. Susie hates for me to touch her, freezes up under the obligatory hugs and kisses. I don't know what shape her skull is under her blow-dried, feathered blonde hair, or whether or not that lump grows at the nape of her neck, too.

Mary's head still looks perfectly round, though. When she came six months ago to tell me in a muttery jumble that she was leaving Fred, needed to go to California to "find herself," could I watch Susie for a few weeks that I knew would turn into a few months or years, she pushed her bangs nervously from her forehead, exposing how her head had kept its shape after all these years. I can still feel that little lump at the nape of her neck, a mound like a small hard candy that no amount of massaging and turning could eradicate.

Using a mirror from my compact, I can see all the way to the back of my bald smooth head: no bumps, no disfiguring irregularities or lumps. I touch the back of my head with my fingertips. If this were a globe of the world, Brazil would be here, snaking down to the nape of my neck. I'm the one with the perfectly shaped head, as it turns out.

A breeze blows in through the window, weaving cool air across the lines and folds in my neck. I bought the house because of this window. "Bill, I want the one with the little porthole bathroom window." He was surprised. Since I retired five years ago and we moved from D.C. to Ithaca, I'd been complaining about living in a cow town with nothing to do. Yet this awkward boat-shaped house wasn't even inside the town limits. Fifteen miles outside of town we found it, in a three-road development of fake colonials and Tudors in a woodsy section near nothing. No church, no shopping mall, not even a general store: just miles of undeveloped land interrupted by the occasional cornfield and dilapidated farmhouse. Not a typical retirement condo, but a real ranch house with real woods conveniently located near nothing at all. Bill thought, what with the cancer and all, that I wouldn't want to be so isolated. "A city chick like you? Alone out here in the woods with beasts almost as wild as those politicos in Washington? What the hell will you do out here?" he teased. But I like it.

Our street is Hunters Lane, no apostrophe. We were to be the flagship street in the Ellis Hills Development, leading an armada of young professionals in the battle to escape Ithaca's burgeoning citification. Ellis Hills was designed to mimic a suburb of a large metropolis, despite the fact that the nearest major city is six hours away and that deer herds are more common than shopping malls in this region. The developers cleared the plots of all the flora and fauna, installing well-trimmed lawns and aqua in-ground pools in the middle of the thick woods.

I like it, this little patch of suburbia nestled in the woods.

There are only fifteen houses in this whole development, and only two on Hunters Lane: our house, number three, and the Schwartz's, number one. The lot for number two was cleared last year. Suburban lawn was brought in on fully-grown sheets, unrolled like wall-to-wall carpet across the length of the property, but the developers went bankrupt last June before the foundation was laid. Black-eyed susans and tiger lilies erupted all over their lawn last August, frosting the green grass with orange and yellow. Now forest ferns are insinuating themselves between the overgrown blades, the earth blossoming back to its pre-development state. Soon the oaks will be back. Were humans bald when they first came down from the trees? I know there were furry apish creatures who awkwardly moved from four feet to two, but I imagine evolving straight from the birds. The wings disappear first, then the beak. After the feathers fall away, it's just a matter of pecking one's way down the trunk.

Every day I put on the blue eye shadow, the orange lipstick, the turtleneck and slacks, pick out a blonde wig and comb it out until static tingles through it. In my mirror, the bald lady stares back me. Every morning for the past six months I face her. With her over-plucked eyebrows arching up to the ceiling, she reminds me of those creepy drawings that pepper cheap children's books. The kind bought at the supermarket to keep the kids quiet while you shop, whose lurid pictures make even Little Red Riding Hood look sinister. Skin the thick white of poached chicken, moon-faced, egg-face. Humpty Dumpty's lipsticked cousin.

I stroke the crown. Head flesh is different from other skin; it's smoother, oilier, stretched taught and firm. It gives a little under pressure. Like a roasted peach, if peaches were ever roasted. I shave weekly rather than face the odd tufts and strands. Better this than the tangled fluff, delicate and nauseating as cotton candy.

I love it here. I mean right here, in this bathroom. The bathroom is unexceptional, except for the fact that it has the same thick gold shag rug as the kitchen and living room. I always hated the cold floor of our old bathroom in D.C. But here I have warm golds, oranges, brown. Even the toilet is golden.

I don't flush. It's my damn house; the down payment came from my mother's paltry inheritance, so I figure I can piss any way I like here. No one comments on the red, darker than menstrual blood, a brick red pool filling up as the day goes by. Usually I give in and flush before Bill and the kids get home, but sometimes I forget.

My window, my lover, my pane. It's not the view I love; it looks out onto the yard, just an overgrown lawn and some scraggly holly bushes we planted one Christmas. It's the window itself that calms me more than all the sedatives and strawberry daiquiris in the world. Perfectly round, filled with thick glass, it is twice the size of my head. The porthole recedes six inches into the wall, leaving a small ledge where I can lean, curving my crossed arms up at the elbows to conform to its shape. The window opens out, so I can rest my arms on the sides even when it's open. The view is nondescript and my position is not particularly comfortable, but everything holds still while I sit at my porthole.

During the winter, the trees that separate our property from our neighbors' go bare. It must happen gradually, but it always takes me by surprise. In summer and fall I look out onto the lovely oak, birch, elm, and then one day at the beginning of spring, suddenly the Schwartz's appears. An ugly house, split level, a bland brown ranch. No glamour, no trim, no style, those Schwartzs; all substance.

Every day I look out my porthole before I get dressed and choose a wig. I stay at the porthole for about the same amount of time I used to take shampooing. I never conditioned, never blow-dried, since my hair fell straight and thick to my shoulders no matter how many eons and dollars were spent on styling. Now I devote the better half of the morning untangling and styling my wigs. I tried wigs made of other women's hair, sold like blood for quick cash at the Red Cross. Real hair, duplicating my hair's ashen brown, just beginning to gray, undyed and uncurled. "Salt and Pepper Fawn," they called it. But wigs are fakes by nature. They prefer to pile mile high, curl too tight, turn crazy clown colors. So I succumbed to their charms, gravitating to the most outrageous blondes, the frizziest curls, the salt-and-pepper zebra stripes. They make my eyes look big, my wigs do.

Outside my window the sun fakes a summer day, shining bright even though it's barely fifteen degrees out. My watch says ten-thirty. Everyone is at school, or work, or shopping.

"It's time," I say to my window, "to face the day." I pop a curly blonde number on my head, not finishing untangling its elaborate zodiac of knots.

Jane

A red beret: that's the ticket. The perfect mikvah outfit.

36

Adding the hat to her red outfit, Jane leaves the house, carefully locking the door behind her. It's a cold spring, a perfect mikvah day. She breathes in the sharp air, tastes wood smoke as she twists an extra-large curl around her tongue.

The monorail is on her end of the yard for once, just waiting to transport her. When Jane had heard that the Walkesons were getting a monorail, she'd envisioned a gleaming silver train floating slowly between their bedrooms, with lots of blue plastic bucket seating and silent air-conditioning. Jane and Mrs. Walkeson would have their own secret room in the caboose, an invisible compartment with red velvet wallpaper and candlelight tucked inside the flashy train. But the monorail turned out to be just a bar with a handle on either side, suspended from a piece of fishing line strung between two trees in the Walkesons' yard. Hopping on now, she squints her eyes until the world blurs. She waits until the last possible nanosecond to jump off, when she's about to hit the tree where the other side of the monorail ends.

She enters through the kitchen door at the side of the house, knowing it is sure to be unlocked. Without taking her boots off, she traipses into the Walkeson's living room, where Mrs. Walkeson is sure to be curled up already in front of the tube.

"Uh, hi Mrs. Walkeson," Jane fumbles. Mrs. Walkeson is asleep on the couch, her head thrown back, eyes closed, mouth open. Her wig is slightly askew, exposing a patch of baby-smooth scalp.

"Oh! Jane. Your dad called earlier saying something about a stomach ache?" She pulls her bathrobe tightly around her, blue peacock, not straightening the wig. A hand reaches out of the robe, grabbing some potato chips sitting in a big plastic bowl on the table near the couch.

"I'm better now. But I've missed most of the school day, anyway." Jane's hand reaches for chips.

She times her crunching to Mrs. Walkeson's. Slouching into the tan modular couches, eyes glued to the T.V., they pick through the tangled wigs slowly, methodically, one clump at a time. Jane sniffs in the musk of the yellow strands, notes of hair spray and tobacco mixing with the dominant scent of burnt toast.

"My sweet lady Anne, I've done what I can," Mrs. Walkeson hums as she pulls the comb through the matted hairs with slow, even motions so as to prevent snarls. "My sweet lady Jane, your servant I remain." The fibers brush against Jane's hand, softer than real hair. Her fingers trace the strands to the roots, feeling for lumps left by the factory glue gun fastening each lock forever to the fabric skull.

"I love the bad ones. The really witchy-bitchy ones," Mrs. Walkeson confides to Jane as they slouch into the overstuffed modular couches, covered up to their necks in acrylic afghans, teasing their way through the wigs. "Now, she used to be bad, really fascinating, sleeping with her sister's boyfriend just for kicks. I missed the episode where she turned good, so I'm just waiting for her to turn bad again." Jane nods, feigning interest in the T.V. soap queens, combing the ears of one of the cats with the wig comb. "Help yourself to some pop, hon. I think there's some cola left in the 'fridge, though it may be flat. Susie is always leaving the damned tops halfway off. If you bother to twist it halfway back on, I can't understand why you can't spend the extra half-second to twist it back on so it doesn't go flat and taste like lighter fluid."

"Can I get you something, Mrs. Walkeson?"

"I'm OK. I'm just going to freshen up in the bathroom."

Jane waits for Mrs. Walkeson to finish, standing in the hall outside the bathroom. One-one-thousand, two-one-thousand....

There's no flush at the end, so Jane is startled when Mrs. Walkeson just appears in the hallway again. Her wig carefully brushed and hair sprayed, the fumes radiating out of the open bathroom door. Jane loves the smells of hair spray, loves its sticky chemical burn in her eyes. Her mother likes to spray the air with hair spray and walk into its invisible cloud. "My beauty mist," she tells Jane as she watches.

She gives Mrs. Walkeson a bright smile and explains, "I've got to go, too," and follows the chemical smell into the bathroom.

Mrs. Walkeson doesn't flush. Sometimes her piss is bright red, as if she'd pissed out straight iodine.

Eager to see what color it will be this time, Jane slips into the bathroom right after Mrs. Walkeson finishes up. Adding her yellow to the red, she plays with Mrs. Walkeson's lipsticks and waits for the orange to form.

If you were a carpenter, and I were a lady, Jane hums as she pillages through the lipsticks, first testing them all on her hand like in a fancy department store before choosing one perfect one with which to coat her lips. She pops the brightest frosted peach deep into her jeans pockets, imagining a secret camera zeroing in on her thieving hands. The eye shadow she powders on up to her eyebrows is public swimming pool blue, nesting in a beach of soupy beige foundation. Would you marry me anyway, would you have my baby. The wigs are piled on top of the hamper, as if awaiting laundry day. Jane sits on the empty toilet, fruitlessly plotting how to snag one, on what pretext could she possibly get her makeup-smeared hands on their snarled yellow curls. Mike's litany pounds in her head as she sits:

You shave your head to keep men from gazing at you after you're married. It's a matter of modesty. You shave your head to prevent the hair from interfering from the mikvah. It's a matter of purity. The law is vague, demanding modesty, purity, separation from men. But how? There is no mention of hair, be it scalp, pubic, or nasal. In all the Torah, usually so explicit on such matters, there is no mention of shaving women's hair. Torah, so concerned with every detail of sex, he says as Jane watches his teeth glinting white and wet in the dark study, is silent about shaving. His tongue gets thick on the 's' in shaving, gives it an extra Hs, Hs, a soft hushing noise. She can see the Hs forming on his tongue, feel it press against his upper palate as he hunches over toward her. Like the refrain of a lullaby the shs sing in her ear when they start reading the Chasidic mystics with their black hats and shaved wives.

You shave your head for pleasure. They say it's about modesty, give you this mishegas about purity, but frankly I think it's aesthetic. His black brows knit together as he sits across from her in the study. It is a wintry Saturday afternoon, and it's Shabbos, so you cannot turn the electricity on or off and as usual he forgot to leave the study lights on before sunset, so they talk in the dark. My theory is, they like their women shaved.

His mouth hangs open a minute as the Hs plays for a full half-note, one beat, two beats, a bark of laughter overtaking it. He rubs his thick mustache as he laughs. A dry, slightly

40

oily aroma fills her noise, quivering the hairs trailing up into her sinuses. The mustache glistens blue black, brighter than his sideburns and outgrown outdated Beatles cut. She could crawl down that throat, huddle between the Hs and soft palate, the fringe of his mustache visible above like the elegant lattice of an upstairs porch. She would shave herself to the bone for that mustache. Poison all the other girls in the sixth grade. Poison everyone with hemlock, sleeping pills, laughing gas, leaving Mike and Jane the only humans left alive.

As she leaves the bathroom, Jane doesn't flush. Instead, she blows a double kiss, like a French lady, kiss-kiss, at herself in the mirror

Charlene

"What's this?"

Jane has already pinned a cavalcade of buttons to her yellow turtleneck. I hate catching kids in the act, hate having to use that cop voice. They don't even have the right to remain silent or demand an attorney; I ask and they must tell. Or lie.

Kennedy For a New America, Clean for Gene, and End the War—Vote McGovern, pinned in a row over her right bud of nipple. Stale campaign coffee from an ancient grey urn, posters mimeographing my fingers purple, knocking door-to-door until I grow what the party pols call "canvassing sores" on her knuckles: the campaigns blend together now. I pick up a "Clean for Gene" button from the bowl of pins

41

sitting on the table. Jane peers up at me, trying to keep a neutral stare, 'sussing out whether she's in trouble. I pin Gene to Jane, careful to place it well above her right nipple. "Jane, what were you up to in the bathroom? Were you frizzing up my good wigs again?" I ask, my eyes staring straight into hers.

"Nuh-uh!"

I fold my arms and stare harder, not telling her to call me Charlene this time. What a little fibber. She stares back as evenly as the meanest soap opera diva. "Hey, we're going to miss *General Hospital*, so put my pins back where you found them and get a Pepsi," I remind her, letting the case be closed for now.

"OK—I'll be right there," she says as she heads for the bathroom to de-pin herself and molest my good wigs. I pin JFK above my right breast and Bobby above my left, just for good luck.

In my breast grow the ducts. Like beads of sweat perspiring beneath my flesh, like grains of sand too numerous to count, like nothing except ducts. I cannot visualize them. Beneath layers of soft fat, smaller than the princess' invisible pea, only detectable by x-ray, laser, microwave. Ducts, flocks of them, waiting like hungry young mouths for the milk to flow. Cancer multiplying like only cancer can.

Goldenrod. Asbestos. Dust mites. These were the plagues I battled with specialists, medicines, shots, unguents. All the while the ducts multiplying quietly, unrelated to my blocked nasal passages, unconcerned with the removal of a small benign cyst buried inside my left nostril. Not just cancer but the ducts themselves multiplied like houses on a developer's road map while the air traveled freely at last each night from my lungs to my nostrils. Above my clean lungs sit my breasts, as smooth to the touch as ever.

Soon my figure will be flat again. A clean slate. To remove the ducts, they must hollow out my breasts, possibly remove them entirely depending on what they find once they put me under and begin to excavate. At night I will finger the scars like nipples, the tissue erect beneath my fingertips. I could never resist picking a scab, always eager to find the new pink skin beneath.

Before I had breasts I had nipples, tan flat orbs as neuter as earlobes. Staring in the mirror, ten years old, fingers circling around the aureole, I'd think of the story they'd told me. The blood will flow, the breasts will bulge, and you will be happy to carry them in front of you. I was skeptical.

I could imagine them only as plastic appendages stuck on to my chest with superglue. I practiced with apples, peaches, enormous yellow grapefruits. Stretching out my shirt, exploding into giggles in front of the mirror, my girlfriends and I parading our fruity breasts for one another. Something made me uneasy as I stared at those perfect grapefruit spheres. We'd never eat the fruit afterwards.

I am just as skeptical about this new version of the story. Just slice off your breasts, chemotherapize your hair, avoid stress and cigarettes, and you'll be just like new, just like you, before puberty. But since I started the chemo, all I've been is sleepy. Every cell begging for rest from breakfast to the late late show. Even after I choke down three cups of coffee two dozen vitamin pills, orange, cranberry, tomato juice, all I can do is plop onto the old gold sofa and wait for the soap operas.

My body feels heavy, even though I've actually lost

weight and am bordering on frail. Not just heavy, but lethargic. What's the right word for it? It's like when I was a kid and I'd swim out at the lake in Saratoga Springs with my aunt and uncle, swim all afternoon, race my brothers, swim underwater with the overfed carp. At dinner it would hit me: this awful heaviness in my bones, as if all the empty space between bone and blood had been replaced by muddy water. Waterlogged, that's what Aunt Louise called it, scolding me for being such a such a tomboy. Don't stay in the water too long or you'll get waterlogged, she'd warn, crossing her arms around her large breasts.

I let out a sigh, letting the air whistle through my nose. My sinuses are clearer than ever; even the goldenrod didn't make me sneeze this spring. For a few crazy days last June I imagined that my allergies clearing somehow triggered the cancer in my breast, but since the chemo started in December I've stopped thinking about cause. The plot thickens, the ducts multiply, the cancer insinuates itself into every nook and cranny like every jilted lover on every soap opera. Surgery seems logical now; I am being carved away like raw marble, waiting for the statue hidden inside to reveal its perfect proportions. Only addition seems impossible: adding food, adding weight, adding any ornament to my body.

I breathe in through my unclogged nose, unpin JFK from my shirt so that Bobby can be the top dog for once, and get ready for my afternoon narcotic, *General Hospital*.

Jane

While Mrs. Walkeson sleeps Jane watches her T.V. It's a big color one, with a special table all its own. Mrs. Walkeson is in a deep slumber in front of the weepy blond girl on *General Hospital*, the gold velvet of the overstuffed couch flowering around her. Jane hates *General Hospital*, especially this annoying blonde girl who bursts into tears whenever Dr. Bob or his evil twin, Dr. Rod, appear. She changes the channel, humming softly to herself, searching for one of those how-to shows: how to cook classic French cuisine, how to fix your muffler, how to raise I'm OK—You're OK kids. Today it's Mr. Chen's E-Z Chinese Cookery. "We're making rice balls, ladies!" Mr. Chen enthuses as the camera closes in on the ingredients. "E-Z, E-Z, right ladies? Go to your kitchens and start discovering the ease of Chinese!"

The kitchen is her laboratory. So different from her mother's kitchen, where milk and meat are carefully held at bay in their separate kingdoms, and organic kosher rules in whole-grained, unpackaged glory. Mrs. Walkeson's kitchen is more like a playground than a kitchen: everything wrapped in bright plastic, mechanical openers and mixers and fixers resting toy-like in their plastic orange green pink blue containers. Extra-large bags of chips bought in quantity at a discount, juju fruits like they sell at the movie theatre but in enormous boxes, and condiments, an array of condiments in glass jars stored in the door of the big yellow refrigerator.

Today it is the condiments that call to her. Sweet yellow-green dill pickles cut like wavy potato chips, unopened translucent cocktail onions in acrid juices, capers from

Spain in elegant miniature glass jars, soy sauce the color of molasses scented with vinegar and ginger, chutney left over from Christmas with a thick mossy mold spreading across the top. The condiments are great for enriching the T.V. chef's recipes. Mr. Chen's rice balls were supposed to be stuffed with chicken and fish, but Jane substitutes chutney and dill pickles, staining the rice green.

"Surprise!" She has to stand right next to Mrs. Walkeson to wake her up. Will Mrs. Walkeson smell funny this time, like a doctor's office flooded with lilacs? Will her wig be off, her scalp raw against the pillow? Crumpled up in the folds of old comforter and gold furniture, she sleeps too soundly, the T.V. and phone never waking her. Her eyes open as Jane pushes a rice ball under her nose.

"Mmm, rice balls. I used to make those when we lived in Washington. One thing's missing," Mrs. Walkeson says as she pushes off the covers. She smells like detergent, a bit too springtime fresh. Jane tries not to stare at her bald head. The wig is off-kilter, tilted to the left, revealing the smooth white forehead beneath. The skin revealed there looks artificial to Jane, too white and shiny. Mrs. Walkeson tugs the wig a bit to the right as she gathers her red satin robe around her and stands up.

In the kitchen, she pulls out a container of coconut flakes left over from a cream pie recipe. "You know Jane," she says as she rolls each greenish ball in the white flakes, "Lately all I want is water." Mrs. Walkeson doesn't even realize that she's been wanting water until the words are already out of her mouth.

"To drink?"

"To drink, to wash, to sleep. I've been thinking that

maybe the water inside my body is contaminated, and that if I soak in some new water, the cancer will stop multiplying. Not very scientific, I know." She sets the balls down on a glass tray, the rice still looking green beneath the coconut flakes, like moldy snowballs.

"Well, I guess it makes more sense than the chemo." Jane puts a whole rice ball in her mouth, tasting the vinegar in the soy sauce against the sweet coconut. She likes to detect each ingredient separately, tease apart their distinct flavors as they blend against her tongue. "There's this old Jewish thing about water healing cancer, especially for women. Let me do some more research." Mrs. Walkeson nods, picking up a T.V. guide. They eat silently, Jane popping the rice balls one at a time into her mouth, Mrs. Walkeson eating the flakes off one at a time, leaving the rice balls green and bare.

CHAPTER THREE:
WEDNESDAY

Jane

Hunters Lane swoops up Hunt Hill, named for the red-suited hunters who make their annual appearances each autumn. It's a small mountain, really, unpopulated and vast. Somebody must own it, Jane knows, but besides these two houses from the failed Ellis Hollow Estates development on Hunters Lane, there is no sign of possession. Hunters overrun the woods behind the Schwartz's property each fall, common as ragweed, and just as irritating. They flash red through the bare forest, never even saying "hello there" if Jane happens to run into them in the woods. She hears their rifles, tat tat tat, all hours, tat tat, all season long. Deer are even commoner. Stags weighed down by their elegant horns, adolescents cantering, jerky and wild-eyed as dope addicts, whole families pressing their noses up against the glass windows in the Schwartz's living room.

"That Walkeson idiot put a salt lick out back by the garbage cans," her dad grouses as they listen to pft, pft of the bullets out back behind the screened glass doors of the kitchen this chilly February morning. "A salt lick, can you believe it? The deer are overpopulating wildly, no natural predators left, stripping all the trees. And Walkeson, the carp-faced idiot, put a salt lick out back. A twenty-five pound salt lick! As if salt would help the poor starving bastards!"

"Salt helps you retain water; maybe the Walkesons thought the salt would help the deer keep from getting dehydrated or something," Jane offers, munching her cinnamon toast and tea, wondering what a carp's face looks like. Toast and tea: no eggs, no dairy, no French toast laden with confectioner's sugar, and absolutely no cereal tarted out in bright pastels. Only dry toast, with a bit of cinnamon, if she begs. And tea: black hot tea, with skim milk if she likes.

After her first and only overnight at the Schwartz's, Susie Walkeson enviously commented, "Your parents are so... European," when Jane's parents served the requisite tea and toast, and Jane doesn't correct her: no, not European, just freaks. After that, any aberration of her parents was easily explained: they're European. I can't watch violent movies; my parents are European. I can't cut my hair short; in Europe, girls grow their hair to their waist. No sugar cereal; Europeans don't believe in it. She starts imagining that her parents are really Europeans, her pretty blonde mother a sophisticated Swede, her swarthy father a passionate Italian. Well, they're the children of Europeans; that's almost the same, she rationalizes, not wanting to think of herself as a liar. Liar, liar, pants on fire, she recites silently, licking the cinnamon off the toast.

"Dehydrated deer! What happy horseshit you're babbling, Jane. Really. Like it doesn't snow every day here? No, not dehydration: starvation. By March, half of them will be dead in their tracks of starvation thanks to our friend Walkeson there..." Her father has launched into his lecture mode, enumerating all the facts and figures regarding local

49

deer population and starvation as Jane sips her tea, humming silently.

Jane closes her eyes and pretends she is in the woods with the deer now, in a forest of dehydration.

Dehydration is her secret weapon. Dehydrated ham, canned peas, soup mix, dried milk, dried fruit, and like the astronauts, freeze dried ice cream. She stores it all high on Hunt Hill, in a Flintstone's lunch box buried in the dirt surrounded by the stones of a crumbling foundation, where perhaps a dairy farmhouse or liquor still once stood. On Fridays, before Shabbat begins, she makes sure to visit her stash, add a can or two to the booty, check to make sure everything is clean and dry, ready.

Every Friday, Jane is one package of Chinese noodles one can of yams one dried papaya closer to flight. Her mother doesn't notice the disappearing dried goods. Mom tends to overstock anyway, in fear of a snowstorm leaving them carless, isolated from the A&P. Soon Jane fills up the Flintstone's box, and has to make do with plastic garbage bags. She takes them into a clearing in the woods she found, twenty minutes away from the house in an area of dense pines. It's a small clearing, ten feet by twelve, laid with large flat stones, a foundation for a house or barn that was never built.

Surrounded by her supplies, sitting on the large cornerstone at the left side of the foundation, Jane knits. Not sweaters, but leaves. As soon as the leaves started turning last fall, she started her project. Using rough yarn that burns into her fingers, she pieces the leaves together. Like sewn to like. Red sewn to red, orange to orange, small to small, oak to oak. Only newly fallen leaves will do, still fired with color; the dry brown ones crumble like soot in her hand. She is consistent, systematic. She uses real knitting needles, but can't manage purl stitches, only simple knitting. At first she thought she'd knit herself some wings, experiment with flight. But now she knows she's knitting a shawl. A mikvah shawl.

A mikvah needs something to cover it. To console it in the dark, after the women have left. Jane can picture it exactly; she's read all about it in Rabbi Loewe. The mikvah attendant sweeps up for the night, switches off the lights, sets the burglar alarms, and leaves the mikvah alone with its two sources of running water and the skin cells of a dozen ovulating women. Its floor grows cold. Unholy.

Without human flesh to absorb the sound waves, the hum of the radiator rings too loud, each clang reverberating off wall upon wall. Perhaps the mikvah hums a little tune, the drips of the faucet in the shower the ladies use to cleanse before they immerse in the mikvah playing against the filling and draining and filling as the two water sources flow together. The mikvah is exposed to the elements, unprotected, chilled by the night air once the ladies' hot flesh disappears for the evening. The mikvah needs a cover.

A leafy cover, not only for the baths, but for the entire mikvah, from entrance to exit. Gold leaves shot through with red, green leaves yellowing at the edges, red leaves, bright as blood. Each leaf absorbing the night sounds of the empty rooms. Jane feels the sound quiver through the leaves, filling their veins, cloaking her mikvah like a soft shawl.

She is Leah. Leah, lover of Jacob, loved by God. Leah, spurned by her Jacob, mocked by Rachel, who everyone knows is her father's secret favorite, Leah will knit the perfect mikvah shawl. As Jane chews her hair she imagines the mikvah cover completed, its leaves glowing gold and red and green, woven together to form a soft carpet over the baths. Leah resplendent with her mikvah cover knit of a thousand and one leaves. Protecting and defending, keeping the golem away, banishing Lilith who steals the breath from babies in the crib, each leaf shielding against the six million lost souls who are too sad to enter heaven. The air is scented with something fresh, a bit racy, like the night air after the last frost melts in early spring.

"Jane! Are you in trance? Earth to Jane! Come on, you space case. Get your hair out of your mouth. And get cracking—you're going to miss your bus."

The white flash of a deer's tail flickers in the woods outside. Jane replaces the hair with toast, grabbing her book bag and lunch box and running for the door. "'Bye Jane. Don't forget to make yourself dinner—I won't be home until late, and Mom has meetings. And wipe your mouth; you've got crumbs all over it."

"Yup."

It is a twenty-minute walk to the bus stop on the corner of Ellis Hollow Road and Route 81, which this far upstate is only a lonely one-lane road. Take Route 81 west, and you eventually reach Elmira, Rochester, even Canada if you drive long enough. Cutting through every major city and town, cleared even in the worst snow storms, it drives through the heart of upstate New York, a long artery linking the small farming towns together to the rusty cities scattered along Western. In Rochester, Ithaca, or Elmira, Route 81 cuts a thick swath across the landscape, running four lanes wide through Buffalo, Aurora, Utica. But out here, half an hour southeast of

52

Ithaca, two hours and twenty minutes from Syracuse, Route 81 dwindles to one lane, indistinguishable from any other country road except for the black and white signs posted every three-quarters of a mile announcing Route 81.

At the corner of Ellis Hills Road and Route 81, Jane leans against the sign. No other kids are waiting; she is either too early or too late. While it takes her dad only twenty minutes to zip her off to school in his VW mini-van, the bus trip is an evil hour each way, lumbering up every backwoods dead-end road, tracing and retracing its path along Route 81 as it picks up every child living in the sparsely populated farmlands west of Ithaca.

The bus is hell in green plastic seats. The boys scream 'fuck' and pick through the girls' purses, digging for Tampax, pulling bra straps, throwing muffins at the driver. Jane ignores the Tampax hunt, ignores the girls, just reads until Margot Wong the Oboe Nerd gets on. Margot Wonton and Jane Schwartz-Warts: look at the lezzies! Jane has perfected the art of ignoring, and the boys move on to a softer, sadder target. She is only bus buddies with Margot; once they're at school, Jane doesn't even look at her. She's at least two castes above Margot in popularity, and doesn't want to squander it. Jane wishes she could always miss the bus. Even Jim the Hippie, who drives the bus every Tuesday and Friday and gives everyone cookies and doesn't allow teasing, doesn't redeem the bus. Not those stinky green seats.

Is she early or late? Jane never wears a watch. "If it isn't sewn to your skin," her mother jokes, "it's as good as lost." Which means it is probably lost, since her mother isn't much one for sewing. Sewing and typing: they're for secretaries, not university department chairs.

Above, a silver plane cuts through the cold gray sky, its exhaust tail dividing the air into two parts, two worlds. Snow flakes down, the small, sparse flakes that fall when it's far too cold for a proper snowstorm. Across the highway the cornfields lie flat, the corn sunk beneath the ground, hibernating until spring. One Mississippi, two Mississippi— she has no patience for Mississippi. When the tenth red car passes, I'll go home, she thinks. A red truck passes immediately: an omen.

She looks down. There are fresh boot prints, probably left by kids running for the bus. She really has missed the bus and should turn around, go now before her father has left in his unheated black jeep for the back roads that take him to his laboratory. Jane spins around in circles to keep warm, stands still and watches the earth quiver as she regains equilibrium. Back, get back to where you once belonged, she sings off key. And she skips back, skips to my Lou like a fifth-grader, her hair in her mouth as she dances back home.

The snow coats the roof of her house, an oversized baby bonnet. From the foot of the driveway, she can see that there are no lights on inside. Dad has already left. Only the front porch lights remain on. The house looks sleepy. Jane palms her bright blue house key in her hand, hesitating. She can't bring herself to disturb the house's slumber, turn up the heat, switch on the lights, run the dishwasher. Besides, she's not supposed to stay there alone. She walks past her driveway, feeling light and free, as if she could go home to anyone's house now, live anywhere, eat someone else's toast and tea like Goldilocks, fight with a younger brother over the last waffle.

Jane starts skipping again, turning up the Walkeson's

well-plowed driveway. She's never rung their front door before; she always comes through the kitchen, which is on the side of the house that faces hers. The door is painted black, with a large number stenciled in white at its center and a large glass window to its left. The window frames the vestibule, empty but for some boots and hats piled in one corner. No lights are on. Another sleeping house, she thinks.

Charlene

It begins in bed. The nausea surges up, overcoming my slumber before the dreams fade. I am awake. There are teeth to brush, urine to expel, breakfasts to make, lunches to pack, and nausea waves through me and I can't move and I wait for awake to end. Drooling a bit at the corner of my mouth. Everything damp. Everything too loud. I cough up some mucus into the silver bowl Bill has left on my side of the bed for the purpose. I burrow back under the covers. Something burns near my thighs and I find my hand there.

Need to find Susie's snow boots. Need to call Dr. S. about the nausea. Need to make a list of what comes next. My hand twists faster, fingers blurring between flesh and cotton. Need a thing between hand and cunt. Need to call Dr. S. Hand clenches it, hand rubs it red, hand wet and stinking with relief. Hand stroking softly now, now. The doorbell rings: Hear the bells chime. The nausea rolls its ragged waves through me and I'm jerking mechanically under the smooth linen covers. The doorbell rings again. It only plays the first four notes of the tune: hear the bells chime, hear the bells chime, the four notes calmly repeating each time the doorbell is pressed. I take my time pulling on a bathrobe, rinsing out my mouth in the bathroom with water, ambling down the stairs to the front door.

"Mrs. Walkeson?"

As usual, Jane Schwartz is underdressed for the weather, wearing only a ski jacket and sneakers, with no hat or gloves in sight. It seems to be a family trait. I've seen her mother jogging in shorts in the dead of winter, I've watched her father shovel snow in trousers and a t-shirt, I've witnessed Jane without hat or mittens, waiting for the bus in sub-zero weather. A cold-blooded lot: doing the minimum of neighborly things, always stressing how busy they are when I call up to discuss the uneven garbage collection service or our ever-soaring property taxes. Not a political bone in their busy bodies: "we're not joiners," Mrs. Schwartz declines politely whenever I walk over with a petition. She is a professor at the University, always racing off in her little red VW beetle. She wears horn rim glasses and ugly brown suits, reminding me of a high-level high school administrator, the sort who only calls you into her office when it's very, very serious. A tweedy, unfriendly lady. But you can't hold the parents against the kids.

"Jane! You must be freezing. Are you sick again?"

She stands in my doorway, her eyes not quite meeting mine. "Well, not exactly. I think I missed my bus, and my parents have already left for work."

"Well come on in. Have you had breakfast yet?" Jane shakes her head up and down, long after she's indicated 'yes.' "I'm kind of under the weather today, so I don't think

I'm up to driving you all the way to school. Should I call your parents at work?" The head nods sideways, even more energetically.

"They won't mind if I just stay with you," she explains. "Since it's Wednesday, Mom should be home by five, if she isn't kept late at a meeting or something."

"Well come in out of the cold, Jane, and we'll figure out something fun to do today. It's too cold to be out waiting for that damned bus anyway; they should close the schools from January to March, as far as I'm concerned."

Her sneakers drip on the gold rug, leaving piss-dark patches. In my bare feet, I carefully wind my way around the dark yellow spots. "Why don't you get yourself a glass of milk and watch some t.v. while I shower?" I suggest. Again the violent nod. I leave her in the kitchen, nose poking into the refrigerator, and head for the bathroom.

The more addicted I become to baths, the less cleansed I feel each morning from my shower. It is the little window of time after the shower that I relish, when the mirrors are steamy, my porthole fogged over so the black tree trunks outside look like the broken brush strokes of an Impressionist painting. There I stand in my blue silk kimono, bald as a Buddha. I wipe off the steam from the vanity, and using a little mirror from my blush compact I shave my head.

I start with the back, sudsing up with soap, the white bar foaming onto my white scalp. An old razor of Bill's, long discarded for some fancy electric model, does the job. The trick is to shave in the direction the hair grows. Like refinishing an old table: rub with the grain.

After the shave, the pills. I open the cabinet, dazzled by the cavalcade of bottles. Cold cream in a large white bottle

57

without a label. Aspirin, extra strength, the kind that sticks in your throat for a long second before it travels down. Half-empty bottles of unfinished antibiotics left over from the last round of family flues. Green cancer pills, violet anti-nausea pills to combat the puking caused by the green pills, pink muscle relaxers, orange pick-me-ups in somber light-brown bottles. My pills, my exotic jewels, too foreign to be appreciated. My riches. I know too well the routine, if not its function: two green, one violet, three pinks, and an orange if I'm feeling woozy. I could necklace them together, design dangly earrings, bracelets, mood rings.

Instead I line them up on the vanity and stare at them. My morning menagerie. I like to take them with the minimum amount of water possible. To feel each catch in my throat, despite the bright sugar coating meant to smooth the swallow.

But today I don't take my pills. I measure out the proper quantities, line them up on the counter, and throw them in the toilet one at a time. Blues, greens, three different shades of pink. They seem so excessive. Cosmetic elaborations that miss the point. Like plastic breasts or wigs made of all-real hair or creative visualization or prayer. I am paring everything down these days. No more elaborations. I pop the fakest, wildest red wig on my head, letting it ride up like a hat on my forehead. I want only fakes now, nothing that pretends to flesh.

"Mrs. Walkeson, can we make hot chocolate?" Jane is in the kitchen, peering into the pantry.

"If you can find all the ingredients. I don't know what exactly we have in there." I watch her pull out the spices, examining each one for hot cocoa potential. Allspice: maybe. Cinnamon: definitely. Pepper: perhaps a dash.

"I don't see any cocoa, but we could melt down these licorice sticks and add some nutmeg." She is already putting the licorice in a small pan, adding pinches of spices. The licorice is the cheap, gummy, artificially flavored kind, formed into thick sticks rather than rope, a leftover from our last car trip to visit Bill's relatives. More gelatin and sugar than licorice, some strange combination of dyes creating a purple hue rather than the deep black I remember from the licorice rope of my childhood, this licorice will add only goo to the hot chocolate. It lacks bite, that sharp peppery zing that is the pride of real licorice.

"O.K.," I tell her, "But don't put too many different flavors in. It's like with water colors: the taste turns to mud if you add too many." She nods, but continues to grab random ingredients from the pantry, the sort of stuff that doesn't even live in the neighborhood of hot cocoa.

The connection between cooking and eating isn't quite clear yet for Jane. There's the initial impulse to cook: a vision of cream-filled, golden baked perfection straight from the pages of *Betty Crocker*. Then there's the strange alchemy of mixing together foreign substances, watching heat change their color, shape, texture, the infinite possibility for gold to emerge from the base substances of the pantry randomly combined. By the time the creation emerges from the oven, the initial interest in the idea of a cake, pot roast, pie has vanished. All the specific images and flavors associated with pie-ness or roast-ness are no longer in play; the main alchemical event ends when her creation comes out of the oven.

Today's concoction is heavy on the spices. Licorice, milk, cinnamon, allspice. Honey, Tabasco sauce, vanilla, granola.

And tea leaves. Tea leaves? "Jane hon, don't you think tea leaves will make the cocoa kind of bitter?"

Jane is opening a tea bag into the pan, mixing the black flakes carefully into the mixture. "They add texture. So is tea really made out of leaves? Like from trees?"

"Yup. I think tea trees are more like plants than trees. They grow them in India and Asia."

Jane ponders this as she stirs, the mixture bubbling up as it boils, filling the kitchen with the scent of licorice and Tabasco. "Do the tea leaves change color in the fall? Is that why there's black tea and brown tea and green tea?"

A forest of tea leaves changing slowly from green to brown to charcoal black. The image is appealing, somehow. "I don't think it works quite like that. We could get a book from the library and find out, though. You better keep stirring that, so it doesn't burn and stick to the bottom of the pan."

Jane stirs some more. I lower the flame, fighting back nausea, thinking of what a mess this is going to be to clean up. "I'm sewing a shawl out of leaves," Jane announces.

"A shawl? Like a big scarf?" I'm trying to picture this, a scarf made only of leaves. I picture Susie and Jane jumping into big piles of leaves in the fall, raking them together in the yard only to leap into the center and scatter them every which way.

"Yup." She's not looking at me. I turn off the heat on the boiler, hoping the stuff hasn't congealed in a burnt mass at the bottom of the pan. The scent of licorice and Tabasco wafts around us. It's a chemical smell, like the deliciously putrid fumes at the gas station.

"Why do you want a shawl? And how do you sew leaves, exactly?"

"Well, you take the leaves when they've just fallen, before they get brown and crumbly, and sew them with regular thread. It's not that hard. I use knitting needles, actually."

"Does Susie help you with this?" I can't imagine my granddaughter choosing leaf-knitting over Barbies.

"Nope. I do it alone."

"But why a shawl?"

Jane hesitates a minute, stirring the cooling mixture vigorously. "You know how we were talking the other day about cancer and stuff? About how you wanted water all the time, to help with the cancer or something?"

Cancer and water. Water and cancer. The words seem meaningless for a moment, like a commercial dancing in my head. "Uh, yeah. I think."

"Do you remember that I told you about this Jewish thing about water? That it's supposed to cure women?" Jane is tasting the mixture, disgust and disappointment registering on her face as the licorice and Tabasco fire up her tongue.

"I think so. Yes." I don't remember, but it doesn't matter.

"Uck. This is gross. Too much Tabasco. Well, I did some research, like I promised you. And I was right: water is used by Jews to cure women of cancer and disease. But we need a mikvah."

"What's that?" I take the mixture and start spooning it into the trash. It's thick and black, like tar melting on Route 81 in August.

"It's a bath, a special bath, that women are supposed to use after, you know, their periods." She can't look me in the eyes when she says "periods."

"Uh huh. But what does your leaf scarf have to do with that?"

"Well at night, when the mikvah is empty, I thought it would need a cover. Something, you know, organic." She is pouring little drops of Tabasco sauce on her fingertips now, and flicking off the hot red drops with the tip of her tongue. Pour, lick, lick, pour. There's a rhythm to Jane's motions, a waltzing lilt. Pour, lick, lick.

"Jane, I'm not even a Jew. I'm barely even a Methodist at this point. What would the other ladies think of me, bald and Christian, swimming around in a mikvah?" I picture myself, shivering naked in a swimming pool, surrounded by healthy, plump old Jewish ladies with big frizzy hair. Despite my doctor's exhortations to explore my "spiritual" side, cancer seems to have made me even more bored with religion than ever. It all seems so ornamental, like that fancy pink icing they make into roses that look so gorgeous on wedding cakes, but tastes like glue. And since we moved out here, it's too long a drive to make on Sundays; the last time we went to church was probably Christmas morning, and I slept through most of that.

"You don't *swim* in a mikvah; you just kind of dunk. But you wouldn't have to go to a public one; I was thinking that maybe we could build you a little mikvah by the sauna." Jane is sucking her hair in quick little slurps now, a bit of drool at the corner of her mouth. I wonder why she doesn't disgust me, this messy unhappy girl. Susie is so clean, so calm in comparison, her blonde hair always brushed, her voice distant even when she's standing right in front of me.

"In the basement? My basement? Why on earth would we do such a thing? I think we'd better stick with hot cocoa for now!"

"It would be easy. We could use an inflatable kiddy pool

62

or something for the base. I have it all worked out."

"But Jane, why would we go to the trouble? Why do I need some Jewish hot tub?"

"Well," Jane says, suddenly all shy, "Well, in this book I read, Rabbi Loewe, who's an expert on mikvah laws, says that the mikvah can help with cancer. Wash your bad blood clean and stuff."

In a flash I picture it: my old blood gone, drained out, replaced by bright red fresh blood pulsing through my veins. The image lingers. "But it's not really my blood that's sick, Jane; it's more like the cells in my body. They've all mutated into cancer."

"Well, the mikvah is supposed to clean out all the impurities in your body, not just in your blood. And it's supposed to help your kid's blood, too, even if she's already born." She is putting all the ingredients away now, haphazardly shoving them into the revolving pantry. "I could build one for you."

I imagine my blood drained out into a vat, replaced with pure spring water. The spring water is then drained out of me into another vat. A tube runs from the vat to Susie's veins. I can't imagine Mary at all in this equation. "I don't know, Jane. How would we even go about building one? Would we do it here, in my house? What would I tell Bill and Susie?"

"You could tell everyone it was a hot tub or something, a special hot tub for cancer patients. It would go with the sauna."

"I need to think about this, Jane." I can see her mind whirring, the hardware spinning as she builds a splendid deluxe mikvah.

"Can we go down and look at the sauna?"

The nausea has subsided for now. I think of the sauna's

63

heat prickling against my arm. I am sleepy again, ready for heat and wet to overcome me. "O.K. I could use a good hot sauna, anyway."

Jane

Taste the air. Taste how its flavor changes as you descend down the staircase, Jane commands herself. She can discern the sweetness of licorice and the burned spiciness of Tabasco in her hair as it twists around her tongue.

Every taste is magnified here in the gloomy dark of the basement. She wills her taste buds to ignore the hair, the burnt taste, the licorice.

Taste the air. Another taste interferes as she reaches the bottom step: the sharp sulfur of rotten eggs. And then, beneath the acrid egg-stink, the sweet moist air.

In the beginning there was water. Endless oceans unbroken by buildings or lighthouses. A world of water, a globe filled with fish. Only the sluggish single-celled organisms living in the depths knew of land, that ugly grey silt mired league upon league beneath the ocean.

Then came the birds, flying out of the water, wings crafted of fins. They were blue jays, common and loud, their wings the color of the sea. Circling in crazy patterns above the water, the birds grew ravenous, exhausted by flight.

The birds imagined trees, land, groves in which to perch. Dry branches for nests. Plants with toothsome nuts. Plump insects crawling on dry earth. And so the tides parted, revealing the grey silt that lay at the bottom of the ocean. The silt turned to mud, thick and smelly. One day passed, two days, a week, a month, and the tides remained parted. The earth between the tides dried in the sun. From seaweed grew green moss. Mice crawled out of jellyfish, lobsters lost their shells and became anteaters, and crickets were heard, throaty crickets singing to the sun. The birds swooped down to investigate.

The land between the tides was covered with green now, except for one small patch of brown mud stinking of sour milk and rotten eggs. Plants and trees were carpeting the green. The jays mocked the mice, chased the crickets, built nests in the trees. Squirrels were seen racing across the green.

Years passed. The tides parted further, the land grew larger, species multiplied. Deer, lions, antelopes left footprints on the land. Still the small patch of fetid brown mud remained. All the animals avoided the mud.

One day a small white she-goat came upon the mud and mistook it for a pond. Being a goat, she was not disturbed by the smell. Being a thirsty goat, she thought she'd have a sip of the mud. As she bent her head to drink, a lock of her white curly hair fell into the mud. The hair twisted and turned, mixing with the mud, gathering speed and size, rolling itself into a large ball. Out of the muddy, hairy mess, a baby human's hand, then face, then body appeared, and rolled out of the mud onto the ground. He was a boy.

The boy began to tear at the goat, pulling handfuls of hair off her to cover his head, his genitals, underneath his arms. He stood upright and strangled the goat. Rain fell, washing away the blood and dirt from the man's body, leaving the hair on his head and genitals and underarms. And so he

65

became the first adult man, Adam. Always the smell of the mud disgusted him. Always he and his sons and his son's sons longed to follow the birds out to sea.

"It smells like rotten eggs down here!" Mrs. Walkeson exclaims as she turns the light on at the top of the staircase, interrupting the story calmly reciting itself in Jane's head. Concentrate, concentrate on the moistness, Jane commands her nose, twisting two strands of hair at once around her tongue, trying to suffocate her taste buds with hair. Taste the air. Taste only its moisture.

One day another baby was found, crying in the mud. There was no goat. She was hairless. A girl. She washed off the mud in a nearby stream, and named herself Leah. And so she became the first woman. The mud did not disgust her.

"It must be from the paint. When Bill got the sauna, he started to paint the basement with this old thick white paint that never quite seemed to dry." In the basement light, Mrs. Walkeson looks especially frail, her skin thin and pale, her frame all bones beneath the bathrobe.

The mud spoke to Leah. "Build a bath to cleanse yourself of me." And so she did. The temples, the rabbis, the laws of kashrut came later. In the beginning there was water. Leah built a pool and every month, after the mud trickled out of her, she dipped under three times: one for each parting tide, and one for the mud left in its wake. Kosher, kosher, kosher, she cried as she surfaced.

From the bottom of the stairs, Jane surveys the debris. Other people's debris, foreign yet familiar. A jungle of broken bicycles, old unpainted doll houses, unlabeled cardboard boxes, and molding records carpet the dank basement floor. After a few minutes, as her nostrils acclimate, the rotten egg smell disappears, replaced by the subtler scent of molding paper.

In the right-hand corner of the large room, the records and boxes and bikes have been cleared away. The sauna stands there like an outhouse, a free-standing edifice, a self-contained, unremarkable box. It has no windows, and is painted hospital puke green. Next to the sauna is a little white card table with thick white bath towels crumpled on top of it. None of the towels look clean. Thick cords wound with silver tape stream out of the bottom of the sauna, twisting around the basement to the one working electrical outlet by the stairs.

"The funny thing about this sauna is that you have to turn it on from the inside," Mrs. Walkeson comments as she clears a path through the broken dollhouses and Chubby Checker records. "I don't know why Bill got such a cheap model. I guess he didn't know if anyone would really bother to use it."

Leah talked to God, chatted with him in the late evening down by the mud. God, she said as she absent-mindedly made mud pies, I've got to do something. I'm going crazy here, what with Jacob ditching me for my sister Rachel.

Build me a shawl, God replied, gurgling under the mud. Weave it from the locks of your hair. Build me a shawl and you shall be purified and perfect and your children shall be purified and perfect and your children's children shall be purified and perfect. Leah scratched her head; her hair was a dull brown color, clipped to her ears. She fingered the straight thin locks of it dubiously. This is not the stuff of ecclesiastic scarves, she thought.

"Damn! Where's that switch?" Mrs. Walkeson coughs

a bit as she fumbles inside the sauna. Then there is silence, heavy breathing. Should she go in, too? Jane wonders. What if Mrs. Walkeson has fallen asleep? What if she chokes on her own saliva? What if she's lying there naked, wigless? Minutes pass. One Mississippi, two Mississippi. Jane taps her foot, standing at the door of the sauna, not daring to enter. The sauna makes a grumbling noise as it starts to heat up. At last, the door cracks open and Mrs. Walkeson appears, fully clothed, beads of sweat necklacing her forehead. "If we bring some water down here, we can make it steam up. It's supposed be good for the pores."

"Is there a hose or something?" Jane asks, still not entering the sauna.

"A hose? No, we have to get the water from upstairs. But there should be a wooden Swedish bucket by the towel rack. It came with the sauna." Mrs. Walkeson scratches her head, making her wig pitch to the right.

"You stay in the sauna; I'll go fill the bucket."

"Okay, Jane. And hand me one of those towels, will you? This robe is getting sticky and gross. The pills I'm taking make me sweat like a sailor."

Leah pulled a few hairs from her scalp, tentatively at first, then quickly, as if plucking a chicken. She lay on her stomach in a grassy knoll on the banks of the mud, and began to knit. Knit one, purl two, she sang to the bluejays. Knit two, purl two. And before seven days and seven nights had passed, she had knit a beautiful shawl, exactly the right size to cover the mud.

"What have you done?" God cried when he saw it.

Leah blinked in astonishment. "Why God, you told me to—"

"I don't give a shit what I told you, Missy! Only God, the great and powerful God, is allowed to create new life!"

"For Pete's sake, God, it's just a shawl—" But even as she uttered the words, she saw that the shawl was moving, growing, rippling with motion. And it was making sounds: little sobs, half-human, half-animal.

Leah grabbed the shawl, unraveled it as fast as she could, and began to swallow it. Enormous mouthfuls of her coarse brown hair filled up her throat to the point of choking. The hair bled a little as Leah bit into it, chewing it up, ignoring its cries, refusing to spit it up. She swallowed it all down until there were no more sobs.

"You're a good girl, Leah. Now, no more monkey business with magical shawls, okay? Leave the creation of the world to me." And with that, God disappeared.

Leah thought that would be the end of it. She still spent her days talking to the mud, though she no longer knit. But a few weeks later, she noticed a lump in her stomach. Must be from eating all that hair, she thought. The lump grew. The blue jays swooped down to investigate. "Pregnant! You're pregnant!!" they cried. And indeed she was.

And that is the story of how Leah became the first pregnant lady.

Jane tries to make her way back up the basement stairs with her eyes closed, practicing for if she goes blind. In the dark, each sound is magnified. The light fixtures hiss like annoyed wasps. Her feet sound like boulders falling down the stairs, no matter how gingerly she walks. Her toes caress each step, feeling up for the edge of the next, and the next. She bumps her head against the door at the top of the stairs, and opens her eyes. Mrs. Walkeson's living room swirls into focus: the yellow couch, the shag rug, the large television on its Formica table, an old red wig piled on top of newspapers stacked up in the corner awaiting the trash. She closes her eyes again, willing her fingertips to guide her to the bathroom. When she goes blind, she will be an old hand at navigation. And with her expertise in blindness, deafness shouldn't be too hard to master. The scent of the bathroom draws her toward it, tickling her nose as she fumbles for the bathroom light.

Old piss and nail polish remover saturate the air. Eyes clenched shut, Jane inhales the artificial bouquet. Exhales. Tastes the air. Tastes petroleum leaking at the gas station, fixative freshly sprayed on charcoal drawings in art class, fast-drying rubber cement in little jars with brushes built in to the tops. A riot of chemical aromas dance on her tongue, playing under and above the lemon notes of the nail polish remover and the dark yellow piss. Perhaps these tangy scents are part of the evolutionary plan, their sickly sweet aroma the candy-coated lure to a new physiology, blood replaced by nail polish remover, lungs pumping out lemony gas. She pictures her healthy blue lungs assimilating these new chemicals, breaking them down, utilizing them to build more durable muscles, firmer thighs. Inhale nail polish, exhale steel. Piss out gold. She is evolving past oxygen, assimilating new neon yellow chemical bonds into her bloodstream with each sniff. Blue lungs will turn green as they absorb the yellow chemicals, a verdant leafy green visible beneath her white skin.

When she opens her eyes, everything is electrified. The shiny metal sink fixtures glitter, catching the light from the overhead lamp. In the mirror, her face glows greenish white, a luminous moon rising over the sink and soap dish. Kiss, kiss. I love you, dahling, Jane mouths as she vamps a movie-star kiss to the mirror. But you need a bit of color, my dear...

Day by day, she hums as she palms a compact filled with three shades of grey eye shadow left open on the counter. Day by day, oh dear lord, three things I pray. To see thee more clearly, love thee more dearly... She can't remember what the third thing is; maybe Mrs. Walkeson has the *Godspell* album around. Jane has never seen Mrs. Walkeson in grey shadow before. Usually it's frosted public swimming pool blue, climbing up to the eyebrow. But here on the counter is a rainbow of grey shadows, accompanied by a thick steel-grey eyeliner pencil precariously poised next to the shadow at the edge of the sink, just waiting to be knocked off, disappearing into oblivion in the wilds of the gold shag rug carpeting the floor.

An easy steal. Day by day, day by day by day... She imagines Susie catching her in the act, her thin blonde eyebrows arching up above her watery blue eyes, her mouth pursing up into a tight condescending button. Jane can see her there, arms crossed, not threatening to tell Jane's mom, not telling her own mom, but instead politely, too politely, suggesting that maybe it's time for Jane to go home now. After all, they're just after-school friends, as Susie often reminds Jane. Susie, queen of the sixth grade. Blonde snotty Susie, made-up in shiny clear lip-gloss and turquoise eyeliner, ignoring Jane in the halls, never sitting with her during lunch. The fastest runner, able to beat even the tallest boy in the 500 meter. Susie with her expensive jeans and skinny wrists, reluctantly coming over to Jane's house on the weekends, only, as she reminds Jane, because there are no other kids to play with

71

out in the boonies and her goddamn grandmother won't get off the couch and drive her to the mall. Susie doesn't steal, doesn't even shoplift at the mall with the other kids; "it's low-class," she sniffs at lunch when the other girls plot a trip to nab some candy and lip gloss from the five-and-dime.

The eye shadow is too easy a steal, Jane decides. Bored, Jane puts it back on the counter. I promise, she says to her image in the vanity mirror, to stop stealing things I don't need. It is only a sin to steal frivolously, she admonishes herself, shaking a finger at the pale girl in the mirror. Mike's is-it-okay-to-steal litany booms back at her:

"There are no absolutes in Torah," Rabbi Mike told her last Sunday. "Even the ten commandments, which the Christians think are so damn immutable, have their little loopholes." The left side of Mike's mouth quivers, the shadow of a smirk appearing as he pronounces 'Christians.' "It's not a sin for a starving man to steal a loaf of bread, says Rashi. Or for a man to steal medicine for his sick wife. The store is closed; the shopkeeper is away on vacation in the Catskills." Mike licks his mouth with the tip of his tongue as he paints the scene, rubs his hands together, oh yes, he can see the whole story unfolding. The light streams in from the window above his desk, the mid-winter glare of a late February afternoon. The light glints off his thick black hair, a million tiny prisms of color shining off the blue-black of his shoulder-length locks. Black absorbs every color. Absorbs her every cell, pink flesh blue jeans red t-shirt brown hair every molecule of color drained away, absorbed into the rivers of black.

"So Jane, let's say the man's wife is one gasp away from death. It's a small town, like Ithaca, with only one pharmacy, Schwartz's Pharmacy and General Store, for miles around.

She's dying of, let's say, hairballs," he says slyly, staring directing at the lock of hair twisted around Jane's tongue, "a clot of hairballs stuck in her stomach." Jane pulls the hair out of mouth, flushing red, feeling the tears begin to sting in her eyes. Don't cry. Don't look at him. Don't breathe. "Only Mr. X's Hairball Dissolvent will do the trick. Schwartz's is closed, there are no pharmacies for miles around, and the old lady is going to die of hairballs if she doesn't get a good swig of Dr. X's Special Extra-Strength Hairball Dissolvent, which goes for about two bucks a pop. Our man happens to have a key to the pharmacy, since he is a former employee of the venerable Schwartz's. He can slip in, grab a bottle, lock the joint up, give the missus a good slug of it, and no one will be the wiser. So, is it a sin to steal?"

Stealing, sin, shul. Today is Wednesday. A school day, and a shul day, Jane suddenly remembers. Wednesdays are shul days, when her mother has to pick her up from school at three-thirty and zoom all the way to Mike's for her four o'clock shul date. Then her father has to remember to fetch her sometime after seven and drive all the way home. Her hand makes a fist around the eye shadow compact. Eyes flit left, right, making the requisite furtive glance to make sure the coast is clear. Her stomach clenches: she can picture her mother parked in her rusting red Volkswagen station wagon in front of the brick school building, waiting and waiting for Jane to appear, her thin blonde eyebrows rising as her eyes close in annoyance. Her dad will forget to call her mom's office, forget to tell her, "Hon, Jane's sick again, some sort of stomach flu, so she didn't go to school, so you can forget about the shlep to Mike's. Do you think we should take her in to Dr. Thomas?" forget, forget, forget, and her mom will be furious.

Should she call her mom now, from Mrs. Walkeson's? She knows the number by heart. 789-8634: ask for Professor Schwartz. She pictures dialing the number, talking to the secretaries, getting her harried mother on the phone. But another picture replaces that: Mike waiting in his study, tapping a pencil in annoyance as the afternoon light fades and it's three-thirty, four, and no Jane; her Mom in the car, tapping her hand on the dashboard, waiting for Jane, scanning the stream of kids racing for the yellow school buses, no Jane; her Dad, ringing Mike's doorbell, Mike and Dad conferring, worried, wondering where she is: still no Jane. She puts the eye shadow compact in her pants pocket, and smiles her most innocent smile at the mirror. I was sick, she'll tell them. I was too sick to remember anything.

But just as she makes the steal, pulls her hand out of her pocket, and alters her smile to look more convincingly sick, something catches her. Yellow glints in the corner of her eye, dazzling her away from the eye shadow.

From the bands circling their ring fingers. From the hoops in their ears. From the holes in their teeth. Melted bangle bracelets, long dangling earrings, thick gold bands passed down many generations in the desert. From a million shades of used gold was the golden calf forged. Day by day the calf grew as earrings, fillings, necklaces were melted onto its body. After seven days, the calf died. Her skin was entirely covered by the molten gold, her pores choking on the thick yellow. She began to rot. The Jewish people danced wildly around her, did Indian woops, sacrificed goats. On the seventh day of the second week the stench was unbearable. "What the hell are you doing?" thundered God, peering down from

Mount Sinai. "Get rid of that crappy old thing. Here, read this and weep." Moses tossed the Jewish people the stone tablets engraved with the ten commandments. They hit the golden calf, splitting it in two, revealing the innards of a small decaying cow. And that was that.

Mrs. Walkeson's wedding ring is a busy affair: a thick gold band etched with diagonal lines forming uneven triangles. Jane fingers it, feels the little planes of brushed metal interspersed with the shiny smooth ones. "William and Charlene Walkeson, July 7, 1945," proclaims the inscription inside the band. A perfect fit: the ring circles Jane's right thumb tight, the metal cool on her thumb, cooler still on her tongue as she licks its uneven surface. With her left hand she reached deep into her red corduroy pants pocket and deposits the ring, while her right hand replaces the shadow carefully on the edge of the sink. An even trade, Jane thinks, mouthing the words to her image in the mirror. Even-Stephen.

Jane hears coughing, constant as an old man's mutter, coming from downstairs. Sometimes Mrs. Walkeson coughs in her sleep, sacked out in front of the T.V. Asleep, yet her mouth contorts with the coughing, as though her lips are trying to wake up her slack sleepy face. What was I supposed to get up here? Jane wonders as she twists the ring deeper into her pants pocket. Water. Cold water. There's a hole, in the bucket, dear Liza a hole, she sings out loud as she fills up the little wood bucket. Day by day, there's a hole, day by day by day.

Charlene

"Day by day..."

Strangers appear in my dreams. The little girl with the flame-red hair in a million spit curls, whispering her most intimate secrets to me. "My left breast is bigger than my right one," she whispers, barely suppressing giggles. The old lady in magenta tights, cursing at me in Spanish. "*Puta! Perro feo!*" An old man with a lazy eye drifting out toward his ear, rocking silently in a chair next to mine. Who are these strangers? Are they dead, seeking out a warm body in which to plant their souls? Or just random images, of no special significance, accumulated from a lifetime of encounters with strangers passed in shopping malls, street corners, public beaches?

As I sleep in the sauna, the heat teasing the water out of my pores, the strangers chatter beneath my eyelids. Their faces, so familiar yet unknown, loom large, particular, detailed. I do not remember much about their bodies. It's their faces, in harsh Technicolor like in the old films, that sit on my retina long after the dream fades.

"Day by day..." the sound of Jane chirping the *Godspell* theme jerks me awake. The little girl with the red curls laughs at me, her big toothy grin coming into sharp focus, then fading as I awaken. I am coughing, my eyes and throat chalky dry from the heat. The yellow light drenches the dark sauna with a golden glow.

"Did you get the water?" I croak, thinking of the steam that will rise from the sauna rocks when water hits them. The rocks are white marble, like lumps of lard that glisten in the light.

"Yup." Jane is outside the sauna door, not looking in through the little window, waiting for me to come on out, fully clothed. I fold the bathrobe back around me, feeling the sweat and flesh itch against the fabric.

"So, are we going to make a mikvah? I can go get the shawl." She's been in my make-up again, the grey eye shadow this time. Smeared up to her eyebrows, it gives her a bruised look. What a ragamuffin. Her long curls frizz at the ends from too much sucking, and her eyes gleam brown beneath the smudges of eye shadow.

"No Jane; I think I'm too tired for a mikvah today; the sauna will have to suffice. Let me add some water to it from the bucket, and then, why don't we have a tea party upstairs, instead?"

"A tea party?" She is two years too old for tea parties, I calculate. I take the bucket from her, which has little smears of eye shadow on the handle. I wonder what the state of my lipsticks will be when I go up into the bathroom. I know I should say something, organize some sort of inquisition about what Jane has been doing with my makeup, complete with a short lecture on respect for one's elders and why stealing even half a breath mint is a Federal crime. But it's more interesting to watch Jane parade around in my makeup, half-wishing I'd confront her. Besides, right now I'm more interested in getting in a hot sauna than interrogating an eleven-year-old.

Closing the sauna door, I remove the bathrobe and coat the marble in water. Like blind marble eyes they stare at me, chipped off from some larger block. Their white gleams as clean as a surgeon's needle. Need to call Dr. S. Need to check my temperature. Need to piss hard without flushing.

"It can be like a science fiction tea party: we can use some food coloring and make purple Venus tea, or yellow and red Jupiter tea. Spaceman tea." I'm improvising now.

"Spacetea. Okay."

Upstairs, everything seems too bright, as if the sun is trapped in the kitchen. Somehow the spacetea ends up taking the rest of the afternoon to concoct, resulting in a multi-colored kitchen and an undrinkable concoction. By the time Jane goes home, I'm asleep on the couch again, the phone calls unmade, the laundry waiting to be moved to the dryer, dinner uncooked.

CHAPTER FOUR:
THURSDAY

Charlene

Bleach, sweat, sleep. The acrid smell is amplified in the darkness. I close my eyes, letting in the sharp scent. Everything is sticky. I should wash off the gummy residue, clean up my teeth and face, restore order, floss. I should at least curl away from Bill's heavy arm, carve my own space in the mattress, separate again.

I've never been able to tolerate an embrace when I sleep. When I was younger, brave enough to pick up strange men in ugly bars but too shy to reclaim my own pillow afterwards, I would lie awake, staring at the odd arm wrapped around me late into the night, count chest hairs like sheep on the torso curled up against mine.

It was in those early days in Washington, when I was Congressman Flint's right-hand girl Friday, when just being a girl with a real job and my own apartment felt like tremendous acts of rebellion. "You were the flashiest gal in a town of flashy gals," Bill always said whenever we retold each other the tale of our first meeting at an unmemorable cocktail party. Little did Bill realize that it was he who inspired my first act of real daring. It occurred that first night when after a few blissful minutes murmuring dreamily under the sheets, I disentangled myself from his resting body, turned to face away from him, and fell into a dreamless sleep. He never felt me throw off his cradling arm from my chest, but from then on, the pattern was set: after sex, I curl back into my own body.

And now, fifteen years later, I am reverting back to my timid ways, lying sticky and awake on my back under that arm, my limbs tense, refusing to succumb to sleep. He is curled up on his side against me, body pressed to body, one arm slipped over my chest and shoulders as he snores, a manacle of flesh.

Although I'm only five pounds lighter than when we first met, I feel weightless, hollow. The weightlessness overcomes me, mingles with the sweat and semen, floats me up into sleep. I still feel the pressure of his hand against my chest, the fuzz of his hairy arm around my shoulders, but now it's a shawl covering me, warming me as I sleep.

The shawl is woven with gold and silver, the threads are molten metal, like silver mercury in a thermometer, the colors soft and malleable as they swirl around me. I have fallen asleep, I think dreamily, sinking deeper into the shawl, under water, the shawl protecting me from the moisture. My hair flows around me, mingling with the threads, weaving its mouse brown into the copper, gold, platinum.

Jane

Nine inches under water, the tight curls unwind. At last: relaxed hair, lolling in thick black lines down her back. Perfect.

Jane's hair swishes past her shoulders in smooth tendrils. 6 a.m., and the house is quiet, folded up for the night. In an hour the morning hustle will begin again: orange juice guzzled down, hair hastily braided, the school bus swimming away from her like a long yellow fish as she rushes after it. But now her body rests, stilled at the bottom of the white porcelain tub, fingertips pressing against the sides to resist flotation. Hold still, she commands her chest, thighs, arms, neck. She holds her breath under the water a second past bursting. Her hair smoothes straight against her skin and everything is still.

In the beginning was water, pure and cool.

The voice booms out from the bottom of the bathtub, a deep tenor rippling the water around her sides. She can't feel the locks uncurling anymore: only the voice, vibrating against her skin. Does water conduct sound? Or do the sound waves just bounce off the water, scattered like droplets? She can't recall.

In the beginning was water. Then woman, then man, then snake, all slithering out of the deep green-blue sea, slapping each other's butts with a spare purple towel.

The towel grew dirty. Soiled from its long days of butt-slapping, ear-washing, and hair-drying, it turned black as the mud at the bottom of the sea.

The voice booms deeper by half an octave as it spits out

the word "mud," the word forming thick and shiny as a late February sun gleaming on an old mahogany table. Rabbi Mike's voice. Rabbi Mike's table.

I don't think there were any purple towels mentioned in the first week of Creation, Jane, she can hear Mike teasing, a smile ghosting the right corner of his lips. Under water his voice rings clear in her ear, as if it is still last Sunday and she is in his study getting ready to go over this week's Torah portion, sitting at the edge of her chair only inches away from his moist red mouth, watching him pull on his black mustache, his thick-lidded eyes dilating from too much Torah study. Aveena malkenu v'shavenu vimru amen. The even, measured voice travels straight from last Sunday to the bathtub, reading aloud the opening mishnah commentaries on Genesis in sonorous Hebrew.

On Sunday she watched the pink in him. Pink pulses through him, tinting his black hair purple, cheeks brick red, fingers sallow orange. In the beginning there was pink. His left hand's fingertips tap on the thick mahogany table while the right hand traces the square of light left by the sun beaming through the window onto the smooth, hard wood. It's not a square; it's got parts, in an L-shape. L for lice, lipstick, Leah. There are no girls named Leah in Jane's class. It lies unclaimed. L, then E-A-H glow in a circle in the well-polished mahogany. Leah, Leah, Leah. His finger traces only the L, over and over, each time a bit more forcefully, leaving a few beads of sweat and skin from which his DNA could surely be decoded. Llll. Tip of the tongue nested on the roof of the mouth, Lllll vibrating through the gums.

Don't squint, Jane, Mike admonishes, finger pausing at the juncture between the two legs of the L. You'll be squinting soon enough once we try to decipher this week's Torah portion. You know, they did this study and found that the lens grows myopic from too much reading, he tells her in the offhand tone that sometimes means he's pulling her leg but sometimes is the cold hard truth. They used Yeshiva boys as their lab rats, and regular goyishe kids who read only cartoons and *Playboy* as the control group. They found that all that Torah reading makes the eye's lens contract like a sea anemone poked by an errant scuba diver.

Her lens contracts sympathetically under water, straining to see through the surface of the water back to last Sunday. He is rubbing his mustache as he talks, the thick black hairs so individual, so distinct beneath his touch. She tries to make out the pores beneath the mustache hairs. He has large pores, his face cratered with ancient acne and stubble, each pore dancing to the surface, cheeks ruddy, as though he's perpetually flushing.

The water grows a degree or two cooler, a breeze from the hallway blows in and then there is no hair, no mustache, no Mike: just skin, smooth cool skin. No roots, no blue black locks glinting in the light, no pores open and red. Only skin, poreless, smooth skin, wrapped tight around the skull. A bald head. Her fingers trace the letters on the head as if it's a chalkboard: L-E-A-H. LEAH LEAH three times she carves using her pinkie nail now her lungs exploding in the cold water eyes grip tighter shut hands clench the sides but she is slipping past last Sunday long black locks starting to curl up against her back again LE, LEA, LEA—

She splashes up. Cool air hits her lungs, the window above the bathtub opening out into the cold March day.

"Jane!" her mother calls, seagull-shrill, from the living

room. "Are you splashing up the bathroom again? I just had Cindy come yesterday to do the floors, and I'm not going to get her in here again until next month. And Jane, you should go back to sleep; Daddy and I want to sleep in."

Jane splashes back down, the water hissing Leah, Leah, drowning out all other voices. Underwater, a window opens in front of her, an oddly shaped hexagonal window with thick glass, the old-fashioned kind that makes the world all soft and hazy. A head is framed by the window. A slender arm sweeps up, stops to stroke the top of the head.

Build me a mikvah, Leah, the voice pounds. Jane feels the head in the window beneath her fingertips now. It is smooth under her hand. Perfectly round. Hairless. The head is completely bald.

Charlene

When I finally awaken again, my mouth is dry and I am light-headed. I stumble out of bed and into the bathroom. Water, water! cries my mouth. I feel thirsty, so terribly thirsty as I pee, my body tightening up as if I can't afford to lose any more water.

Bill is gone. The house is too empty, too quiet. And too dry, the heat blasting silently into my pores. The dream swims back to me as I sip a glass of tap water in the bathroom: something about shawls, hair, death, baths.

I should perform the morning routine. I should shower, dress, comb out a wig, pop it on and go shopping for groceries at the P&C, the big one, with lots of fresh baked goods, off Route 79. I should get up, get dressed, assess the needs of the pantry, make a list, get in the car.

But I am paralyzed, the satin silver and gold threads of the shawl—or was it my hair?—still palpable beneath this waking day. I can't see them, but I feel them in the air, like dust mites or microscopic germs. Slender threads, wrapped around me, metal. Hair or shawl, which was it? I can't recall; the dream scoots away like an Olympic swimmer passing me in the pool, rushing ahead of me. I'm all mixed up, I think as I brush my teeth. Is it the chemo? No. It's that Jane Schwartz and her mikvah talk, mixing me all up with her Hebrew bathtubs and shawls.

After such a strange dream, I need reassurance, I decide. The measured gaze of a mirror, perhaps, sizing me up. The mirror above my vanity will not do; no, it's not quite the ticket. I make a face at my face in the mirror. I don't want a regular mirror, with its Technicolor photorealism. Instead, what I really want, I decide as I move to my window, is the offhand reflection of a windowpane. My porthole window is exactly right: the glass is so thick that everything is distorted, the edges blurred, the world reflected in optimistically broad brush strokes. I stand a foot away, facing the window, so that it can reflect my whole body. And I stare.

"Jesus, Mary, Joseph! I look like a pin-head," I call out, my voice groggy, the first words of the day coming out loud and chirpy. I clear my throat, and look again. I really do look like a pinhead. Tall, broad-shouldered, long-necked, slim-hipped: these are the familiar geographies I see as always reflected back at me. But this head! When did my head shrink? I've looked at my head plenty since I went bald. But never have I noticed the strange proportions, the uneven pyramid, the pinheadyness of my new figure.

Six months since I first went bowling-ball bald, shaving off the ugly, uneven cottony fluff that was left after the first round of chemo. "Better bald than Bozo," I joked to Bill. Standing right here at the window, I took Bill's razor and sheared it all off, not bothering with soap and water, enjoying the nicks and cuts. I don't know why I didn't use the vanity mirror. My head seemed enormous as I ran the razor over the fluffy mess. Back then, I was accustomed only to seeing my face exposed, not this circular globe of flesh. Perhaps I was so focused on the task of de-Bozoing, eliminating the strands left sticking up off my scalp, that I was only looking at my head, as if it were unattached from the rest of my long-limbed body. The sight of my scalp was a relief: there it was finally, smooth, clean, dignified after so many months of ugly red patches of flesh and clumps of hair stringing off the comb each morning, tufts of it left like cat hair on my pillow each morning. A relief, to finally be rid of it all. Now, my head seems so small, like a sallow tennis ball stuck on to the long bony stalk of neck.

Adrenaline pulses through me again. I need a project. Will Jane come over again, fake-sick, full of plans, ready to knit a shawl, build a mikvah, have a pedicure? I put on an auburn wig without combing it, leave the window, and find some juice tucked away in the back of the refrigerator. I need a larger head if I'm going to fight this cancer business. I need a smaller body and larger head and lots of water.

Exhaustion wafts back through my veins like a drug. Perhaps it is actually the effect of a drug, one of the dozens I popped before bed last night. I'm too tired for the trek to the P&C. The dream swims back: the threads of the shawl, gold and silver; my hair, all curly luxury. I drink orange juice, straight from the carton, and watch, as my ghostly green reflection drinks, too, in the avocado sheen of the refrigerator.

Jane

Small, so small.

Jane sucks her cheeks in and stares at her pale face in the bathroom vanity, tracing the width across her chest with a forefinger.

"Jane? What are you doing in there, drowning? I need to shave. If you're not going to school, you can wait until I shave to take your shower."

She looks at the face in the mirror, not answering. A small, sallow face peers back.

Minuscule. A gnat, a sparrow, a little imp, a bat. When they shop, Jane's mother can't help exclaim over her tiny waist, her little matchstick legs, those delicate arms. We need the smallest size you carry; we're all petite in our family, her mother explains to the salesgirl, who grunts in disinterest and gestures toward the juniors. No no, she's too small for a junior's petite four. We need the girl's sizes, maybe a ten? Or an eight? And do you have a children's shoe department? Her mother always forgets Jane's shoe size, assumes it's a good three sizes smaller than it actually is. They can't be a women's six; they're long, but so narrow! so slender! And oh, those gorgeous high arches. Any ballerina would kill for them.

"Jane? I'm not kidding. Get the hell out of the bathroom. Now!" He is banging on the door now, jiggling the door handle.

Jane likes to measure herself. Not her height, which is just an abstract number, like the atomic weight of helium or the distance in kilometers to Jupiter, but the space. The space left between her thighs when she clenches her legs together. The space hollowed out above her sharp collarbones. The space she takes up on the lunchroom bench. Is she taking up more today than last week? Than yesterday? She measures the distance from the left edge of the bench to the right edge of her flesh, makes a little nick on the Formica marking the outer limits of her thighs. On the way to Hebrew school she measures. How much room is left in the bucket seat of the car after she nestles in? Was there more space on the tan squishy plastic last week? At home she measures each limb separately, how many fists long or wide it is, is it getting too big. Her arms are too long, reaching down toward her knees, well past her waist.

"Clasp me," she commands her father every morning before breakfast, when her stomach is empty and flat. He seizes her waist with his hairy hands, lacing his fingers together. She likes the feel of it, the automatic way her chest tightens and breath quickens. His fingers macraméd together like a lacy belt, her waist tight and small. "You have a wasp waist, you little bumble bee," he murmurs as he squeezes, and she laughs, loving her small buzzing body, so small, so agile.

But he's angry now. After she relinquishes the bathroom, after they eat toast and tea together in silence, after she silently nods when he asks if she's still too sick for school, he leaves in the V.W. Beetle without clasping. Her stomach grips as she listens to the car pull out of the driveway. She doesn't eat the rest of her toast, throwing it into the kitchen trash, watching it turn from food to garbage with just the flick of her wrist, sliding off to join the other ex-foods.

As she hops the monorail to Mrs. Walkeson's, hanging on to the wire contraption lopsided, with only one hand, she fingers her ribs with the other, sucking her stomach in. Jumping off the monorail, running towards the kitchen door, she keeps her hand on her stomach, feeling it flat and smooth beneath her hand, stroking it like it's her favorite cat.

All morning, she keeps her stomach flat. She watches it as they watch the soap operas, lifting her shirt up when Mrs. Walkeson isn't looking to survey the taut flesh, making sure it isn't puckering up around her belly button.

But by lunchtime, her stomach is expanding with air, pressing out over her red pant's elastic waist. Mrs. Walkeson flits around the kitchen. Jane is playing Deaf-Mute today, and only nods when Mrs. Walkeson speaks. Mrs. Walkeson knows about the Deaf-Mute game, and even will play it herself sometimes, if Jane keeps it up long enough.

"You eat like a bird," Mrs. Walkeson comments as she dishes out some cream of tomato soup into a yellow bowl.

"I'm sick," Jane replies, breaking her Deaf-Mute silence. Jane fingers the sharp edges of her collarbones, imagines the bones hollowed out, ready for flight. Mrs. Walkeson is so skinny. Her cheekbones push against her skin, nearly pressing through to the surface. Jane's face lacks bones. She squeezes her cheeks, the fat little circles of flesh; she pinches them pink, and imagines how Mrs. Walkeson's cheeks might

89

look if accented with the expensive blush Jane has stolen from her bathroom vanity. There is no extra flesh to measure on Mrs. Walkeson. Her skeleton seems ready to pop out of her skin, pressing to the surface. Below Mrs. Walkeson's collarbone, the delicate bones of her chest form a stepladder down her sternum. They ripple when she moves, fan out beneath her chest as she stirs the soup, adjusts a stray wig hair, clears Jane's dishes.

"I'm finished," Jane declares, pushing the soup aside.

"But you never eat enough. You eat like a bird, a starved sparrow, and then you get sick all the time," Mrs. Walkeson sighs as she scoops Jane's unfinished soup into the garbage. Jane nods a vigorous "no," puffing her cheeks out like a stuffed pig until Mrs. Walkeson laughs.

If anyone resembles a bird, it's Mrs. Walkeson, with her long neck and fluttery hands, her plumage of red, yellow, or jet black curls rising above her scalp. Not a sparrow: something colorful and exotic, rarely found in the sky: a peacock, a pair of lovebirds, a pink flamingo. No: a great blue heron. Mrs. Walkeson in flight, a blue wig high on her head, twiggy arms flapping, against a full moon, white light streaming through her bathrobe, revealing all the hollow bones in her body. As she swoops up, she smiles out into the night, her curls drifting up into the clouds, higher, higher.

Jane shakes the image out of her mind. It's time to get to work; the mikvah shawl needs measuring. In fake sign language, she tells Mrs. Walkeson that she's going back to her own house to take a nap.

"Okay, little deaf sparrow. If you're really going to go to sleep, I guess you can go home. But don't use the stove or anything until your mom gets back, and call or come back over if you need anything." Jane nods "yes" and runs through the yard back to her own house.

The red front door is hard to unlock. "Damn!" she screams as her key fails, "damn damn damn!" until the lock gives and she is home.

Inside, the dark blankets the vestibule, the coat closet, the light fixtures. Everything coated in darkness, even though it's only early afternoon. Everything stands too still.

The bathroom is the darkest of all. And warm, heat radiating up from the basement boiler directly below. Racing into the bathroom, turning on no lights, there is no noise except her footsteps and breath, heaving in out in. It's mikvah time, she tells the pale face ghosting her in the mirror. Time for the mikvah shawl. "Damn!" she yells into the mirror, "Damn damn damn!"

She runs in the kitchen grabs all necessary supplies yells damn damn damn and heads outside, careful to lock the sliding glass doors behind her so that her mother won't have an opportunity to lecture her about ax murderers when she gets home.

Outside, it is the first of March. The snow melts beneath her heels as she makes her way up Hunt Hill. "Beware the Ides of March," her father quoted at breakfast, while Jane ignored his rambling recounting of Brutus and Caesar and the rest. Now his words sing in her head as she trudges through the woods: beware the Ides, beware the Ides, beware the Ides of March.

Making her way up Hunt Hill, her sneakers sliding into the muddy ground, she clutches a jumbo-sized box of Oreos, unopened, seized from her mother's pantry. Dessert. Spelled with two s's, because you want second helpings. It's a perfect addition to the cereals and pickles and biscuits she's been stockpiling: the first high-calorie sweet, a good choice for when the healthier provisions start to dwindle away. Beware the Ides, beware the Ides: just as her feet are refusing to walk any further, she reaches the clearing.

The bottom of her roofless stone hut has turned to mud. She inspects the damage, opening each bag, pulling out a purple magic marker to mark each item like a meat inspector stamping a beefy carcass with USDA APPROVED. The Flintstone's lunch box has worked, protecting the pickles and cocoa and dehydrated noodle soup from the muddy ground. J, she writes on each item, not caring whether the ink takes or not. But one bag, the biggest of the lot, overflowing with individually-sized portions of rainbow-colored breakfast cereal she's stolen a six-pack at a time from the Walkeson's, one flimsy bag that was too big for the Flintstone's lunch box and had to live in its own plastic garbage bag, one damn bag is torn to pieces. The paw prints in the mud beside it indicate that this is the handiwork of a diligent raccoon. Damn raccoons. If she lives in the forest, they will be her competitors, sworn enemies, potential dinner entrees. Raccoon steaks on the grill, and a Daniel Boone cap twirling on her head: yes, she can almost feel the weight of the fur, the tail tickling her neck. She grinds her heel into the paw print until it vanishes.

Hungry, she opens the Oreos. When she runs away, she'll have to make each Oreo last a whole day. Three square meals must be carved out of each one. She inspects each cookie, checking for symmetry, thickness of cream middles, and any breakage in the chocolate outsides. The third one is especially flawless: no cracks, no extra creme. She lays it out on a leaf, blows away any excess invisible crumbs, and measures.

Her thighs are three perfect Oreos wide. The distance between kneecap and waist is seven and one-half Oreos She tries to break the cookie into thirds, but it crumbles, and the white cream filling smears all over her hand. She runs through the barucha for blessing food in her head. Baruch atah adonai blessed are you oh lord our god king of the universe for giving us bread vimruh amen. Her tongue licks in delicate sweeps across her hand. And stops, the white cream poised on the tip.

Before me you shall cover your head. Before eating you shall honor me.

The prayer, the words Mike has taught her to say each time before she eats, Mike's voice, swim back through her ears in a jumble. Religious Jewish men cover their heads to demonstrate that we are always in the presence of God, whose force could rip your scalp right off. It's like a big condom against God, Mike has told her: you never know when you might need to protect yourself, since He is always around us, everywhere all the time. Everywhere all the time: Jane can't picture this; it's too vague, too threatening to be believable.

As she sat across from him last Sunday, the lights off, the room cold, she felt Mike's voice fill the room. Closing her eyes for a minute, concentrating on his baritone, she let him conjure up a clear image of this everywhere all the time God. And especially at meals you must honor God, Mike's voice commands, remember His horrible force, cover your head, offer prayers, hope He lets you swallow another bite on this green earth. Every Jewish man must shield himself from this awful force, like Abraham, like Isaac, like Jacob did.

93

"So why don't women have to protect themselves?" she had asked, opening her eyes suddenly, the room deliriously bright compared to the darkness beneath her lids. "If God is everywhere, dangerously close, an incendiary blaze to be avoided, don't women need protection, little caps or something, as well? Since women fix the meals, you'd think they'd be especially worried about God stalking them, burning through the roofs of their kitchen, messing up the soup."

"An interesting point," Mike allowed, eyes meeting hers, locking in and burrowing down like ice picks. "An interesting point. Women only have to light Shabbos candles and make babies; it's men who must negotiate with God. All prayers are optional, extra, for women."

Mike's lips seemed so pink last Sunday, the color of a new piglet, and just as soft. Aren't purses made of pigskin, or pig's ears? She imagined a tiny purse made out of his blushing lips, a zipper joining them together. "What about mikvah?" she asked, feeling those lips close around hers.

"Mikvah? You mean t'aanit niddeh, family purity. Mikvah is just one aspect of it," he replied, tongue outlining each lip slowly as he rambled his mikvah litany.

You must not enter the mikvah until you have been completely clean for seven days. But what if you thought you were clean, find no spots on the pad, no blood in your underwear for seven days, and then on the eighth, there it is, a big red splotch? You've already gone to the mikvah, cleansed, purified. Your eye revealed no impurity, but there it appears, after the fact, and after the mikvah waters have cleansed you. Are you purified still?

The rabbis are tormented by this. By the inexactitude of it, the tendency for little pink drips to spot up the panties with no warning. Shammai says, "For all women it is sufficient for them to reckon uncleanness from their time of first discovering a flow." But Hillel replies, "They are deemed unclean retroactively, from the time of examination, at which the flow of blood is discovered, to the last examination made at which no flow was discovered." So what do we conclude? Has she "validly immersed," as the rabbis so legalistically like to put it, or has she just contaminated the pool, her husband, her future and present children? What if the blood only appears after she's already gone to the mikvah? Her intent is pure, but her underwear is not. And there is no external system for verifying her purity: she is the only judge here, the final arbiter checking, rechecking for blood. In a way, Mike suggests with a sly smile, she is god here, the only and ultimate mikvah judge.

Of course the woman could lie, pretend not to notice the errant spot appearing days after she's already gone to the mikvah and screwed her husband silly.

"Maybe this," Mike said, black eyes inflamed, leaning in towards Jane, tilting his chair precariously off the ground, "maybe this is the primal scene of Jewish guilt! A hundred, two hundred generations of women faking it, pretending to clean undies, risking, or so say the esteemed rebbes of yore, the physical and moral health of both past and future generations!" The pink lips twisted at the sides, a smirk and a smile battling for supremacy across his face.

Jane twists her own lips into a smirk-smile, feeling the muscles tense. She swallows the Oreo whole. Liar, liar, pants on fire. She imagines a parade of naked women lined up, underwear in hand, bringing them to Mike for weekly inspection.

She imagines herself lying without hesitation to Mike about it, swearing high and low that her underwear is a pure and blameless white. Jane likes to lie. To her mother, to her teachers, but most especially to Susie. Playing truth or dare with the lights off. Waiting for Susie to ask again, "Truth: do you have, um, hair, you know, there?" And every time Jane shrieks, "Ooo how gross! No way, José!" careful to conceal the curly black wisps under thick cotton undies, careful not to ever, ever let her towel drop after they shower. When she gets her period, she won't tell. No one will see, no one will know: she'll be the only witness, watching the blood come out in—how does it flow, in spurts or streams?

The sky is suddenly onyx, shifting from day to night without a pause for twilight, as it does in early spring. Jane takes two more Oreos from the bag and gobbles them down. Bags and more bags: she digs through a pile of plastic bags filled with supplies, looking for the mikvah shawl.

"This place is a mess!" she proclaims out loud. As she takes out the mikvah shawl from its blue plastic bag, she can feel how dry the leaves have stayed, unmolested by the melting snow. She runs her fingers across them: too dry, in fact. No needle will be able to knit such parched skin. She has lied to Mrs. Walkeson, promised a beautifully knit shawl when all she has are these dry leaves. Liar, liar, leaves on fire.

It doesn't matter; there's no such thing as a mikvah shawl, anyway, she imagines telling her. I made that part up. The mikvah is the point, the real thing. But still she sees Mrs. Walkeson in a pool of water, covered by a leafy shawl, protected from God's wrath. Tears sting her eyes as she starts to crumble the leaves in her hand, one at a time. No shawl will ever be made of these leaves and Mrs. Walkeson will freeze from the cold of the mikvah's waters, burn with the fire of God's dark eyes upon her. Mrs. Walkeson, skin blue, wigless, her delicate bones unprotected in the mikvah.

Tape. I can tape the leaves together. Her eyes dry up, the salt leaving a tight, plastic feeling. No, not tape. Glue! I'll glue gun the bastards, she says aloud, her father's bluster lacing each consonant.

CHAPTER 5:
FRIDAY

Charlene

The swing set sprouts like an ugly weed in the Schwartz's front yard, a sprawling green eyesore. Why don't they get rid of it?

Jane certainly isn't swinging. From my porthole window, I can see her, crouched on the ground beneath the rusting bars. There aren't even any swings attached to it, just seatless chains. She's hunched over a blue object I can't quite identify, legs stretched out long in front of her, chest caving over the mysterious blue thing in her lap. Her hand reaches up to finger a broken chain hanging above her head. It's a depressing scene, really.

She's sucking her hair now. Her position shifts; I can see that the blue thing in her lap is a book of some sort. Poor kid. Even when she's alone, reading to herself, she seems to bristle with anxiety. Should I go outside, invite her in, rescue her from beneath the broken swing? Tell her to take that hair out of her mouth—does she want a tree to sprout in her stomach? Pull her nose out of that book? She's such a furious reader—flipping pages back and forth, craning her head into the book until it practically falls right in.

Outside, the light is fading. It must be hard for her to

make the words out, the early spring day brushing dusk against her pages. It's almost time to make dinner; too late now to go out and ask Jane to come over and visit me.

What time is it? I pull myself away from the window and look around for my watch. It's 3:30; I've let a whole day pass, doing nothing but staring out this damn window. I scratch my head in annoyance, and realize I'm walking around wigless, balder than an egg.

Geez Louise, I think as I plop an uncombed curly blonde wig on my head. I'm turning into a freak. Soon Jane will be the only one who's weird enough to tolerate me!

I heave my body down the stairs. Do something normal: start dinner. Set the table. Comb your wig. No, that's not really normal. Turn on the T.V., preheat the oven, wash your hands.

As I soap up my hands with a little dish-washing fluid in the sink, a voice sings around me, a luminous halo of sound swishing around me as I scrub:

Leah, Leah. Build me a mikvah.

The voice has a ringing quality, halfway between a bell and a voice, circling around me as I rinse off the green dishwashing fluid from my hands.

And then my hands are clean and the voice is gone. I am alone. The house is silent, but for the buzz of the heating system. Everything is quiet. Everything is normal. There are no voices.

I flip the little black-and-white kitchen T.V. on and start setting the table for dinner, enjoying the uninteresting sounds the china makes.

Jane

The mikvah can only be entered at night. This way, the woman's privacy is protected from the casual observer, the man on the street.

Under the swing set in the front yard, on the sloping hill that follows the driveway up toward her house, Jane reads Rabbi Loewe's words carefully. Without swings, the swing-set looks unfinished. Its rusting bars stand like the skeleton of a mansion, abandoned before completion.

The mikvah can only be entered at night. So the night sky, emptied of color, will be our only witness. This is the law: no exceptions. I will follow every mikvah step exactly, she promises herself silently, read all the directions twice, no mistakes, no monkey business. Mrs. Walkeson's mikvah has to be the real thing, not some stupid kid version. She reaches up and pulls on the seatless swing-chain, feeling its iron press cold upon her hand. No monkey business.

Jane abandoned the old green swing set last summer. All in one rainy August week she turned eleven, the seats broke, and the orange rust began, spreading fast like lichens through the whole metal frame. No more swinging, she thought to herself the day after her birthday; you're eleven now.

Now, as she stares up at the seatless chains, Jane remembers rising up to the clouds, the feel of the metal between her fingers as she gripped tight, the soft flight her body made as she jumped off. She would talk to the sky as the swing carried her, sing swing songs to the clouds, catch me, catch me if you can.

But she is reading now, not swinging. It's dumb kid's

stuff, really, especially this old swing set her father planted in the yard three summers ago when they first moved in. Stupid kiddy stuff. Besides, the set is all rusty, orange and green eating up the shiny silver metal frame. Can't you get some kind of disease from rust?

She turns back to her book, reading Loewe's emphatic words: the mikvah may only be entered at night. What was it Mike said about that? She struggles to recall Mike's words last Sunday about privacy, mikvahs, cleanliness, what was it again?, trying to remember so she will have something smart to say back to him this Sunday, something extra-clever. She fingers one of the broken, rusty swing chains dangling above her head, worrying it between her fingers as she sucks a single strand of hair, a lone light brown strand streaked by last summer's sun.

The secret state. That's what he called it. It's not her period that is the secret state, Mike had said, one side of his face twisting into a half-smile. Not menstruation itself, but the delight to follow. For immediately after her mikvah, she is supposed to, she is commanded to, she is... he searches for the right word, his hand gesturing in the air, tufts of black hair sprouting on the tops of the fingers, *compelled*, to fuck her husband again. Total cleanliness, every cell scoured, followed immediately by total sex, Mike told her, his mouth pausing to shape the words "total" and "sex" in his mouth as if eating Belgian chocolates, carefully nibbling so as to taste each rich bite. *This* is her secret state: she is primed for fucking.

But this isn't what her book says. The law of the mikvah protects the woman's modesty, says Rabbi Loewe primly in chapter three. She goes at night to keep her private matters private. No one except God should watch her.

She has him spread open on her lap, the blue cover cold beneath her hands. Sitting cross-legged under the old, broken swing set, she reads fast, swallowing down all the words at once. Maybe Loewe and Mike are actually saying the same thing, different ways. Is "keeping modest" the same as keeping a secret state? She twirls the hair around in her mouth with her tongue, as if she can twist the answer out of it.

No one needs to know that she is good and ready to fuck, Mike told her. That's the deal: the rabbis want only her husband to know when it's time. But she gets her own pleasure out of this little ritual, gets to live in—what did Mike call it?— a 'liminal' state in the mikvah, suspended between pure and impure, between sex and abstinence, life and death.

"What's liminal?" she asked Mike.

"Figure it out from the context: we're talking about the space between two extremes, man." He waved his hands up in exasperation. There are only a few hairs on each of his fingers, but they are long and thick, like cat's whiskers.

Jane still isn't sure about what liminal means exactly, or how it relates to mikvah. She sighs out loud, letting the hair fall away from her mouth as she exhales, and turns back to her book. Rabbi Loewe is silent on the husband part. And on the liminal part. The law is clear, he intones across her page: the mikvah should be entered at night, to protect the privacy of the women.

Alone, in the dark, they enter. And exit. Is it scary, walking at night to the mikvah? Do they keep the lights on all night, just in case someone shows up? Do they ever lock the doors?

Close down for the holiday? Who runs the mikvah, anyway? And couldn't somebody follow her there, secretly spy on her, watch her walk from home to mikvah, hiding under the same dark sky that is supposed to protect her? Jane imagines Mrs. Walkeson hurrying along the road in a trench coat and blonde curly wig, horror movie music rising in the background like in *Halloween*, the camera moving in, closer, closer...

Jane flips through the pages, looking for other evidence of Mike's claims about the sex part. She finds the bit she's looking for: Purity—Abstinence.

Originally only three days of abstinence beyond her actual blood flow were legislated; it is the women, they say, who campaigned for a full week free of sex. Rabbi Loewe quotes Rabbi Akiva: "As it is written: 'the women desired a longer period of separation.'"

As it is written: what a strange phrase. Who talks like that, "as it is written."

As it is written. She wonders who wrote "as it is written" first. Mike might know. Or he might just make it up.

She can barely make out the words on the page now; the sky is suddenly a soupy gray, darkening fast. There is no twilight tonight. She lets her eyes go to soft focus, blurring the page into Mike's remembered voice.

Yet the law is the law, however obscure its sources, Mike says whenever she asks why we even bother with this crazy stuff: kashrut, mikvah, torah, shul. It's misheganah, she says, shaking her head, repeating her father's favorite phrase: the whole lot of it is mishegas. She loves that word: from mishegas: nonsense or crazy talk, to misheganah: a crazy thing or person. I'll teach Mrs. Walkeson the difference between mishegas and misheganah before we do the mikvah,

103

she promises herself.

But the misheganah, crazy part is the whole point, Mike insists. Its inexplicable, incomprehensible, illogical basis is its force, its godliness, what sets it apart from man. Though written by men, the law is inspired by God. Its insanity is its holiness, what separates it from us. Division. That's the key to it, he says with a smile. The laws of separation: clean from dirty, holy from profane, woman from man. Which implies they are not self-evident, these elemental differences. Or logical.

Yeah, yeah, she thinks as she flips around through the dog-eared pages of Loewe, nibbling on a pinky nail, then on a large curl that's resting on her shoulder, frizzing at the ends. The sky is turning a watery, dark gray now. It's been overcast all day, getting gloomier and grayer as the afternoon slides away and the glare of winter light fades to a mossy black. The words swim around the page, all the numbers ordering the laws and Rabbi Loewe's careful explication blurring into one.

A noise starts to hum in her ear, its source inexplicable. She closes the book, listening closely. It as if her ear itself is buzzing, humming an indecipherable tune, la la lee laa lay la, modulating up and down, the words and rhythms changing every time she seems to catch them. An ungraspable sound, slipping through her eardrum. It's God, she thinks with absolute certainty.

God buzzes. His voice fills up the rusting bars of the old swing set. The swings are gone; only the chains that used to hold them remain, suspended from the frame. Their iron chain-links clang against each other, shaking in time to His buzzing. Standing up, brushing the dirt off the butt of her jeans, Jane checks her digital wristwatch her father brought back from Japan, pressing the button that lights up its blue face. It is 6:15 p.m. and Jane, still damp from her bath, hair freezing in the March wind, stands facing the swing set while God buzzes and the sky turns a chilly gray.

She pulls herself up onto the crossbar of the "A" on one side of the swing set, hoists her legs to standing, then pulls up onto the high bar, until she is sitting dead center, with one set of broken swings beneath her on either side. She looks toward the sky. It's a cloudy day, the darkening sky still white with clouds, the sun setting into the haze, like a flashlight aimed at a cup of milk.

On top of the swing set, perched on the high bar, she listens. Wasps cavort around her, buzzing an octave above God's baritone. Get up, lazybones, the wasps tell her. She is not afraid up here. The two A-frames stand firm at either end, connected by the high bar, with the broken swing-chains hanging down in straight lines like a difficult geometry problem. On top of the world, on top of the world, she sings, drowning out the wasps. How do wasps live through the snow, the cold, the bitter wind?

She lets the book fall to the ground. To hell with Loewe, he's just a ham, she sings, even louder. I don't give a damn, for Rabbi Loewe.

She stands up, the bar, the swingless chains, the ground, the grass all far below her. Tip-toeing like Nadia Comaneci on the balance beam, nothing breaks her focus, nothing sinks her back to earth as she makes her way along the bar, hands extended sideways for balance.

He hums, loud at her ankles in clusters of wasps. Leah, he calls in his husky voice, Leah my girlie where is my mikvah?

I'm trying, God, she calls back. The bar wobbles as she shouts. But I need glue to make the cover.

The cover? God asks, buzzing louder, an angry cloud of wasps circling in around her left ankle. His voice is rising now, angry that he is being angered. Who said anything about a cover?

Look up, she commands her head, look high at the clouds the trees the sparrows anything up not down. If her eyes leave the sky, the ground will pull her down. Tumbling like a small town newspaper's lead story-child falling into a well, she'll fall, tunnel down at a sickening speed. Don't think of falling, she admonishes herself. Kiss the sky, make the girls cry, sing and sigh, she sings up to the darkening clouds. Kiss the sky, kiss the sky, build a mikvah for Mrs. Walkeson and sigh, oh me oh my.

A wasp lands on her left sneaker, cross-pollinating the laces. She glances down at the wasp, jiggles her foot to brush it off. It stays fixed to the lace, resolute. The ground leaps up at her and her head swims high.

I know your laws, God. I know about the family purity, the shaved heads, all that stuff, she whispers. Her balance is perfect. She straightens her back, eyes toward the sun now, walking across the high bar in her heavy blue sneakers as if she were on solid ground. I know all your laws. But the mikvah shawl is mine. I won't make the mikvah without it.

The sky darkens, the wasp buzzes off her sneaker, the ground swirls up again. God hisses through the metal bars, his voice echoing as if he were driving through a tunnel. Leah, Leah. I need my mikvah. Build me my mikvah and I'll let you make any sort of cover you want.

Dinner.

Diiiineeeer.

Another voice sing-songs a few notes above God's, until God has faded back into the early March buzz of the wasps.

"Diii-ner" her mother calls from the door, using her cattle-round-up call that always annoys Jane. "Jane, get down from there before you break your neck. We really need to get rid of that eyesore. And for God's sake, take that hair out of your mouth."

She hops to the ground, feeling flight and gravity argue a moment before she hits the earth. I need a plan, she thinks. I need to stop God's goddamn buzzing. I need glue, I need the mikvah cover, and I need the mikvah. All through dinner, all through school, she plans.

Meanwhile, God buzzes.

Make me my mikvah, he buzzes. Make it now.

Charlene

The silver utensils sparkle like gems against the soft damask tablecloth. Setting the table: I must be the only woman in America who enjoys this mundane ritual. Tonight, I top it all off with the two silver candle holders, the heavy ones from St. Louis, and light two long white tapers.

I stand at the head of the table a moment, watching the candlelight flatter the china. Everything is so carefully arranged, like a Zen garden, the circular shape of the plates contrasting with the sharp lines and angles of the silver cutlery. On Fridays, no matter how sleepy and sick I feel, I still make a special effort to set a good table.

Tonight, I've ironed the blue tablecloth and napkins smooth, like I used to iron the crisp blue seersucker suits the men would wear to church when I was a girl. In St. Louis, it wasn't considered proper to change after church; whatever you wore Sunday morning stayed on until after Sunday supper, so seersucker blue would drape the whole day.

St. Louis Sunday Dinners. What a production they were! My mother gave them that name. She dressed the whole house in blue and white for the occasion: blue tablecloth and white taper candles for the old oak dining room table, blue suits with crisp white shirts for the men, and blue-and-white patterned dresses for the ladies.

Everything had to be specially decorated for our St. Louis Sunday Dinners. First, in the morning, we'd help her iron the mens' suits, stretching the pants legs flat against the ironing board like insects pinned and preserved in an ideal form. Then, she'd iron our blue and white crinoline pinafores as soon as we got back from church, smoothing out the wrinkles acquired through long hours of hearing the holy word. Finally, she'd "fix us up," starting with me because I was the oldest. After much cheek-pinching, hair-brushing, and face-scrubbing, she'd look at her handiwork, sigh, and start all over again with my hair, trying to coax some spit curls out of my bangs. My hair was so stubborn. All her spit, hot irons, rag curlers, round iron curlers, and Vaseline couldn't convince it to curl. After spending what seemed like hours on my hair, my mother would finally give a loud sigh, brush it up into a ponytail, and wrap a thick blue velvet ribbon around it all.

Meredith was next. Meredith didn't need much fixing.

I'd sit on an old chair covered in pink silk and watch while my mother did her hair. Meredith's hair was blonde, and though it didn't curl, at least it glittered a bright yellow gold. My mother ran a comb through her hair, pinned one front lock to each side of her head, and Meredith was done. "Two curls up," my mother called it, though there weren't any curls on Meredith's head. Finally, she'd hastily fix her own hair, twirling her bangs around her pinky until they bounced like tiny springs. Then she'd place a small blue cap on top of it all, with three bright turquoise feathers.

At our St. Louis Sunday Dinner, all the women would wear some variation on a bright blue dress. I don't know if it was family tradition or the remnants of some obscure Methodist religious practice, but blue was mandatory for Sundays. The men filed in for dinner after talking crops and cattle shares in the parlor, each in a dark blue seersucker blazer and heavy black shoes, the smell of shoe polish casting a masculine aroma on the fussy pink parlor. I loved that smell. The women would still be upstairs, gossiping, spit curling, and giggling in my mother's sitting room. She kept sugary brandy up there, and would serve it to the ladies in pale pink teacups. Her sitting room would soon be awash in pink and blue, the ladies' skin glowing bright, the night a fading blue sea out the French windows.

When Sunday supper was finally ready, Lucinda, our cook, would ring a small silver bell. We would never hear it upstairs; with the door closed, my mother's sitting room was like a remote pink island tucked away inside the house, sound waves reaching around rather than entering its pastel domain. Removing their dark blue hats, the men would shuffle up to the table, and my father would yell "Mary!

Meredith! Charlene! Lucinda says the dumplings are ready!"
And down we'd come, my mother leading a coterie of
women freshly powdered, curled, and gossiped. Grace was
said, then chicken, lamb, ham, and soft corn muffins made
the rounds. The room would glow blue, like the inside of a
robin's egg, as the long white candles inside the heavy silver
candle sticks lit up blue clothes, blue tablecloth, blue twilight.

I don't know where my mother got the candlesticks. Were
they a wedding gift from her Charleston clan? A rare store
purchase, perhaps from Carson Pirie Scott, "my Carson's,"
as she called it, in Chicago? Or did she inherit them from her
own mother, my long dead-in-childbirth Grandma Dixon?
They were unusual: thick silver engraved with swirling
shapes reminiscent of Arabic lettering. They were much larger
and heavier than the dainty cutlery found on our Sunday
table. My mother never spoke of them. She wasn't one to tell
stories about household objects, unless they were somehow
linked to her glamorous adolescence, her life before us as the
belle of all of Charleston's balls. She was raised a Charleston
girl. I was named for Charleston; I would have simply been
'Charles' had I been a boy. "So you're a Charleston girl, too,
just like me," my mother always told me, but I didn't believe
her.

After her death not a year after Bill and I got married, my
sister Meredith sent me a small package, unlabeled, no note
or other identification, no return address. Only the name on
the address, Miss Charlene Lindenson, clued me in to the
origin of this package. Only my family in St. Louis would
still address me by my maiden name more than a year after
I was married. There was no note in the package, but it was
well-packed, a month's worth of the sports pages of *The St.*

Louis Post-Dispatch rolled over and over the objects inside. News of the high school hockey team's winning streak made me homesick as I unraveled the layers of newspaper. I knew it was from Meredith, because she was always the organizer, and a good present-wrapper, too.

She had sent me three of my mother's belongings. Only three. I don't know why I expected more. The house was to remain in the possession of the family, tended by Meredith and her husband, so there was no need to get rid of Mother's household knick-knacks. In fact, I don't know why they even sent me the candlesticks; perhaps they were tired of them. They didn't really match the rest of the house.

She had sent me the candlesticks, a small hand iron, and a cameo brooch of carmine and ivory. I immediately pinned the brooch to my dress, admiring its carved orange face engraved in white ivory. I didn't remember my mother ever wearing such a brooch, but my eyes teared anyway. What other secret, elegant possessions had she kept hidden from us?

I stored the iron in the kitchen, under the sink. An old-fashioned iron, so heavy to mail, useless. What would I ever do with that?

And then I held the candlesticks, one in each hand, feeling how heavy they were, fingering the engravings until they pressed red lines into my flesh, as if they carried a Braille message only my fingertips could decode. I carried the candles to my dinner table, and through three houses, two forms of cancer, a daughter, and a grandchild, there they have remained. I still call them the St. Louis candlesticks, even though they're far too heavy and ornate for most St. Louis folks.

Tonight, they need a bit of cleaning, their swirling patterns darkened by oxidation. It's moist in my house; all the silver oxidizes quickly. Since I got sick, I haven't kept up. Most of the silver is packed away in the closet, resting there, unused since we moved out to Hunters Lane. Perhaps I'll take it all out and have a silver tea party with Susie or Jane. They would like the whole process, the polishing with stinky chemicals, the soaking, the rubbing, the old toothbrush used to get the dirt out of the tricky places, then the tea and sandwiches with the crusts removed. Jane especially: she has that intelligent patience, the desire to see how things work, how we get from dirty silver to high tea. Susie would only be interested in the party.

The candles have burned down a few inches. The day is turning, the night casting its quiet gaze over the afternoon. Five o'clock already, time to take a quick bath before Bill and Susie get back from soccer practice and we finally eat. I've been staring at these damn St. Louis candlesticks for an hour now, as if they were talismans, treasured family heirlooms. But they're probably not that old; just some store-bought American extravagance of my mother's, her notion of a rich lady's finery.

I stand by the candles, looking out the dining room window into the woods as the grey sky turns a dark silver, like the silver jar of night cream my mother ordered annually from Paris. It came in a dark, yet untarnished metal jar, made of a sort of black silver that I've never encountered anywhere else. It held only a few ounces of pink lotion, which my mother was careful to make last a full year. She'd pat a minuscule amount of it each night beneath her eyes and around her neck, carefully screwing the jar's lid back on tight once she was finished. The silver jar of night cream, silk stockings delivered from Chicago each month, her weekly bath of fresh milk and honey. "Your mother's extravagances," my father called them.

My mother's small extravagances. My father had no extravagances to speak of, and no real wealth, either. He did well enough to support us in his burgeoning St. Louis insurance business, but didn't own property beyond a few acres surrounding our house. In St. Louis, wealth is things: cattle, crops, houses, not abstractions like insurance.

The night has turned completely black now. Outside, my yard is invisible, erased by the dark. Pitch black, tar black: the night sky thickens as I gaze into it. And silver. More silver glitters in my mind's eyes as I stare. Silver claws. And the blinding blue water.

Silver claws supported the body of my mother's bathtub. There was only one bathroom for everyone, located in the upstairs hallway between my parents' room and my mother's parlor, and one bathtub. But even though everyone had to use it, it was my mother's bathtub.

The tub was something to see. It was enormous, big enough for a grown man to stretch out comfortably. Crafted of bone-white porcelain, it crouched on ornate silver claws. Each claw clasped a silver ball, giving the tub the appearance of an overweight bird that had swooped to the ground to grab its prey. A heavy, old-fashioned beast it was, squatting there in the center of the room. The white bathtub stood free in the middle of the gleaming white tiled bathroom. Like a giant bird it roosted, the feet tarnishing each day to a shiny bronze. My mother detested bronze. Bronzed silver, faded blues, graying whites: these were her sworn enemies.

113

The moisture in the bathroom left the claws in a state of perpetual tarnish, giving my mother cause for a weekly round of silver polishing. I hated the rotten-egg smell of the polish, loathed how it would get under my nails, settling in beneath the quick, reeking for hours afterwards no matter how we scrubbed. The silver claws of the tub always carried that awful smell with them; as we bathed, the odor would waft up. They were ugly, those claws, especially the talons, curling around the silver eggs. They reminded me of the evil, carnivorous birds I'd read about that snatched small children away.

My mother loved her bathtub. Each Friday, she'd give Meredith and me one new rag a piece, and march us up into the bathroom, to take on one claw each. That way, each claw got cleaned bi-monthly. As we worked on the claws, she cleaned the rest of the silver, bringing the fancy cutlery, the black-silver jar of French night crème, and a silver necklace with a small silver swan hanging from its center into the bathroom. Sometimes my mother would let me count up how many pieces of silver she had, how many forks, spoons, knifes, sundries. "You have thirteen silver tea spoons," I would announce, the number blooming in my mouth like a bouquet of wild flowers gathered especially for her. Surrounded by her silver, sitting beside us on a pale blue bath mat, she hummed her favorite tune, "Daisy, Daisy, give me your answer true," as she scrubbed the silver. We'd join in on the chorus, "A bicycle built for two," giggling at the thought of such a contraption. I pictured that bicycle cast in silver, an ornate machine as difficult to clean as the bathtub talons. Finally, my mother would stop singing, stop cleaning, and announce, "Time for a bath, girls," and we'd abandon the claws and go downstairs to the kitchen to boil water for the tub.

Because it took so damn long to boil enough hot water to fill the tub, baths were not an every-day affair. Despite the talons, I loved taking baths. I especially loved the color the ordinary tap water would turn in the tub: turquoise blue, as if sky had been poured straight in. As I soaked up the hot water, lying flat in the enormous, quiet pool, I finally felt still.

But cleaning the tub's talons was an awful chore. It was like giving a dragon a pedicure. Cleaning between the claws was the trickiest. The claws were fused to the silver balls in some places, while they curled over them in others, leaving a small gap between the underside of the claw and the ball. Kneeling beside the bathtub, twisting an old cloth up tight to fit, I'd angle my rag a hundred different ways, hoping my mother would decide that it was time for our bath.

I was crouched over the claw when the blood started. I stood up, dizzy from the acrid scent of the silver polish. To steady myself, I gazed down at the hexagonal white floor tiles, hoping their even shapes would steady me. Instead, what I saw there made my head swim.

Stigmata, I thought. Like the saints.

Clumps, not drops, of a purplish blood were smeared on the tiles. Wasn't there one saint, Theresa maybe, who bled and bled until she died? We weren't Catholic, or "Papist," as my mother called it, wrinkling her nose as she spat out the word, so all the saints were a foggy, bloody blur in my head. But a Catholic girl at school had a book with a saint for every day of the year, with black-and-white woodcut prints illustrating each saint's torment, suffering, and death. I'd only seen this book once, but I loved it. At night, if I couldn't sleep, I'd think of myself as a black-and-white woodcut print, being eaten by a pride of lions in Jesus' name.

Who starved, who bled, who was flayed alive? As I stared down at the blood smears so bright against the white floor, the silver polish fumes tearing up my eyes, I tried to sort out my saints. Who burned, who was devoured by lions, who was shot full of arrows until he looked like a pincushion? As I wiped the blood off the floor with my polishing rag, my mind made a woodcut of each: Theresa, Francis, Christopher, Sebastian. Saint Sebastian, with a million black arrows piercing his milky skin. New drops of blood appeared on the floor, thicker, darker blotches of it falling too quickly for me to wipe them all up. Maybe God was piercing me with invisible arrows, punishing me at last for my hidden sins. What a relief, I thought as I rubbed the talon with my cloth.

Just then, I heard a voice buzz, the same voice I heard earlier today when I washed my hands in the kitchen sink. The voice rang in bell-like peals:

Leah, Leah, Leah....

and then nothing.

A second before my head hit the floor and everything went black, I heard Meredith cry, "Good grief, Charlene! You've gotten the Curse all over the floor!"

Jane

The woman who chewed off her own fingers. The baby born with two hearts and no liver. The man whose eyes closed up, never to re-open, on a train from Calcutta to New Delhi, some infinitesimal ant or organism—Jane isn't really paying attention and can't tell whether it's bugs or microbes he's on tonight—making mincemeat of the poor shmuck's eyelids.

At dinner, it is Diseases of the World Night. Fridays are family night, the one night all week when her mother cooks, and her dad leaves the lab early to join the family for dinner. Sometimes they light Shabbos candles, two long white tapers in clear glass candlesticks that burn straight through dessert; sometimes they forget. Tonight the candles are burning unevenly, one flaring up high, flame an angry red. Its long taper is reduced to a short white stump by the time they've eaten their salads, while the other burns a slow, cool yellow. Jane's dad chews faster with each disease recited, his whole face glowing with joy at disease and dinner. Eggplant parmagiana mixes with elephantiasis, e-coli, Tourette's syndrome.

Glue is the ticket. In the middle of dessert, as she swallows down orange sherbet swirled with raspberry, the thought arrives, clear and fully formed: glue.

Glue, thick and sweet, emitted in orderly globs from the mouth of the gun. As her father rambles on about Down's Syndrome, she can see the neat, oval pearls, one-quarter inch apart, glistening between the leaves, binding tighter than Abraham's covenant with God, tighter still than the tightest spit curls her mother used to make before Jane started sucking her hair. Perfect pearls, sticking each leaf to each, gluing the shawl together. A superglue-coated mikvah shawl, letting no foreign particles enter or exit. But how to get the glue gun, wrest it from wherever her father has buried it in the two-car garage? She twists a lock from the back of her head around her neck and into her mouth, trying to think of how she can make him lead her right to the glue without spilling the beans about her mikvah plans.

"Daddy, can we do a project tonight?" she interrupts.

"Maybe, if you stop that disgusting habit and eat some real food for a change. Do we have any kits left?"

Damn. No kit.

Knot a beaded headband using only rope, beads, and your own sailor's knots; tie-die as many t-shirts as there are colors in the rainbow; bake sugarless, flourless banana bread just by adding your own water and organic bananas: these are Jane's favorites. Bought on a whim, appearing for no special reason on Sunday mornings, after bagels but before shul, when only Jane and Dad are awake. He loves to decipher the poorly-worded directions, to laugh as Jane points out their horrible grammar, to let her do the mixing and measuring, to scour the house together for that missing final ingredient they always end up lacking. Kits for instant home biospheres, a miniature model beehive, an army of wooden soldiers whose faces they paint over with peace symbols.

"You're not buying her more of those plastic kits, David. They're as bad as Barbies!" Her mom's eyelids are closed tight, eyebrows raising up to her unbleached blonde widow's peak. They all know the sigh will be next. "Uuff. I wish you would buy her less junky presents, if you're going to waste all that money." Her mom will buy any, all, every book for her, from adult soft-core romances to African fairy tales to who-killed-JFK rants. But not Barbies, Star Trek outfits, or crafts kits.

"Daddy, I think we have one left: the passive solar doll

house, the one you got in Japan or, or Finland or somewhere." Passive solar will do the trick, Jane reckons; after all, their whole house was redone passive solar last year, each window painstakingly removed, replaced with green-tinted solar cells. Now it's cold in the house, the sun not beaming enough solar power into the cells to last through the cold Ithaca spring.

The cells of the house: their building blocks, the DNA. He's taught her all about cells, both human and architectural. He loves passive solar almost as fervently as he loves DNA, spliced and diced in his laboratory. Lovely two-toned DNA, twisted around itself, the secret code, the truth found in the cells of your toenail, the tip of your nose, your calluses. Of course he knew that in Ithaca with its eight-month winters and rainy summers there isn't enough sun to keep the house warm all year, so two black Franklin stoves complement the solar cells, and everyone wears extra sweaters and pretends that it's warm enough. "Denmark, not Finland," he corrects. "We'll take a look at it after dinner."

In the garage, after the dinner dishes are washed, they set up shop. A small corner table is loaded up with the goods: the solar dollhouse kit, a set of screwdrivers with a rainbow of head-sizes, and the glue. An oversized bottle of craftsman's glue, extra-strength, unopened, perfect. In its brown translucent bottle it glistens like molasses, honey, maple syrup. The ideal condiment.

The mikvah will be built of cool white marble, the shawl a silken cover of fine leaves and glue. Jane can see it so clearly: Mrs. Walkeson floats up from the bottom, new hair visibly sprouting, pale yellow curls glowing bright against the dark leaves. She rests on the top, floating face down, breathing in the water, every cell cleansed and calm, the shawl gently covering her, keeping her warm. So clear, so lovely. It's hard to believe it isn't already built.

But first, the glue. Everything depends on the glue. Glue by glue. Jane hums the *Godspell* theme as they work, substituting "glue" for "day," her father dissolving into laughter each time she repeats it. Glue by glue. Oh, dear Lord, three glues I pray. The story of glue, of Leah and the glue, she silently recites as they work:

In the beginning there was glue. Leah sipped it from enormous orange poppies with the blackest of seeds. Soon, Leah began to refine her glue, mixing poppy juice with horse gluten, making the strongest, thickest glue around. She pasted her sister Rachel's thick black curls to one another. Ate cups of it, consumed huge, brown Mason jars full as she watched Jacob make love to Rachel, to the servant girl, to a whole harem of servant girls in transparent scarves and gold lamé bras.

You see, Leah had been married for a year or so, and still hadn't managed to get knocked up. Only when she got him shit-faced drunk would Jacob make love to Leah. Even then, he often stopped mid-screw, exhausted, sweat dripping off his thick black mustache, pulling out of her into a deep, dull sleep. But he was always in the mood for Rachel. Leah sulked, watching him with Rachel, changing their love-stained sheets every Sunday.

God, Leah whined, dear God, if you won't make Jacob stop loving Rachel and start loving me, can't you at least knock me up? Hmm, God thought; there's a challenge. So God knocked up Leah once, twice, three, seven times, rehearsing perhaps for his future career with Mary.

Meanwhile, Rachel was barren. No matter how many nights she spent with Jacob, no matter how long she propped her legs up after the act, feeling his juices trickle down her, she was out of luck. Leah gained a new beauty with each pregnancy, her round face glowing, her breasts bursting with milk. Rachel, on the other hand, grew bitter. It was as if all Leah's unhappiness had been transplanted to Rachel. The more Rachel and Jacob screwed, the more kids popped out of Leah. "It's Jacob's fault," Rachel pouted to whoever would listen, but Leah's extended belly and shrieking pack of kids bespoke otherwise. Barren bitch, muttered the servants under their breath.

It was not God who Rachel turned to. No, it was Zephiniah, her beautiful dark-skinned servant girl, Zephiniah, whose firm limbs and huge smile always brought a lusty glow to Jacob's visage.

"Zephiniah, go sleep with Jacob. I won't be jealous," Rachel promised. Zephiniah couldn't believe her ears, for Rachel had always been harsh with her, making her do the dirtiest house work, always quick to keep her out of Jacob's sight. Zephiniah was a young girl, a Canaanite captured in the latest internecine battle between the tribes. So into the bushes went Zephiniah and Jacob, and soon enough, Zephiniah was chock full of baby, her stomach protruding out of her slender frame. But when the time came for Zephiniah to give birth, Rachel thrust Zephiniah between her legs, glued their legs to one another's with Leah's special orange poppy superglue so Zephiniah couldn't escape. "We'll see who gets to be the mother of this child," Rachel chortled, knowing that by law whatever came from between her own legs was rightfully hers. Zephiniah clawed and wailed, but what was she to do?

121

The glue was too strong to escape. It had a resiny smell, a thick perfume that wrapped around Rachel and Zephiniah.

Glued tight, Rachel pulled the baby out of Zephiniah's crotch, and forevermore claimed the baby as her own. Zephiniah, bloody and raw, weeped, screaming for Jacob, begging him to intercede, prevent Rachel from robbing her of their baby.

But the glue held, the baby was born, and it was Rachel's. All mine, she crowed. They called him Gad, which means "good fortune," and always the resiny smell of glue permeated his breath. And when his wife gave birth, many years later, this child too smelled of glue, for Rachel had altered the whole family's DNA with her glue experiment.

And that's the end of the story of Leah and the glue, Jane announces silently to herself, coming back to the task at hand. The glue coats Jane's fingers as she pieces together the kit. She loves this glue glove, the second skin that forms over her own hand.

"Daddy?" she asks, looking up into his eyes narrowed with concentration. "I think we're missing some of the panels." Sweat crawls down his brow, across the wrinkles his face makes as he works. He wipes his forehead with his hand. The glue coats him, too, his bristly arms hairs stiffened by it, sticking out like a porcupine's quills.

"That's impossible, Janie." By undiscussed decree, he is the only one she allows to call her 'Janie.' "Look—four panels for each side of the roof, containing six cells apiece. That's how many cells total?" Jane's eyes roll and then cross.

"Twenty-four, duh. But we've only got twenty-three." The twenty-fourth cell secretly photosynthesizes inside her jeans pocket, energizing her whole torso.

"Let me count."

And then a few seconds later, "Shit. You're right. I'll have to see if I can get a makeshift cell from one of the botanists across the hall at the lab. I should be able to tweak a regular solar cell down to size..." His eyes narrow further: he's already in the lab, consumed by problem-solving, the game of it, the garage and kit now a million light years away.

Jane stares into his grey eyes, watching him tunnel away, and snatches the two remaining bottles of glue, right in front of him. Gotcha.

CHAPTER 6:
SATURDAY

Charlene

The thought flashes, as if someone else is having it:

"The ducts are multiplying."

My eyes open and the clock flashes red six forty-three, six forty-five. I awaken with Bill's arm still planted upon my chest. The arm is hot and sweaty. As I close my eyes again I can feel the tiny ducts multiplying.

A new creature is forming beneath my hairless skin. Ducts replace skeleton, blood, cartilage, water. They link together, redesigning my body's internal architecture. No bone, no tissue, no skin: a structure made only of ducts, infinitesimal vessels formed to carry other materials, transport rivers of mucousy lymph. A body of canals.

I didn't even know what ducts were until I was diagnosed with lymphoma. When I was nursing Mary, my eyes would freeze tight when the other moms would yammer on about ducts and nipples. I didn't want to know the messy details. The act of nursing was already perfect. I didn't want to clutter it up by learning about how the dutiful ducts help the milk to travel to the nipple, conveying it along like a microscopic dairy factory. I never knew that a conveyer could cause so many problems.

But now, the ducts multiply, go haywire, grow like radioactive corn in a '50s sci-fi thriller. Watch out! The ducts are multiplying! Duck and cover! Perhaps after the ducts are through with me I'll have three legs, seven eyes, no breasts. A series of lungs. A new, stronger heart with eighteen ventricles. Or perhaps everything will be reduced, simplified: one of everything. A breast, an arm, a single ventricle pumping oxygen in and out of the heart.

The ducts are multiplying. I feel oddly light-hearted, as if good news had suddenly been wired, like in an old movie: "Telegram for Mrs. Charlene Walkeson! Your rich uncle died, and has left you a million bucks!" Perhaps cancer is a form of evolution, all those wild mutant cells exploding into new life forms. We'll slither out of our old lumbering bodies into lighter skins. Or we'll lose brain matter, gain tumors. We'll become lumpier, less anxious creatures. Perhaps I am the first of a brave new species, an evolutionary breakthrough. Perhaps I am completely losing my mind.

Red six-fifty, red six fifty- one: it's almost time to get up and face the day. Bill grumbles, muttering to some unseen ghost, flopping away from me so at last the dead weight of his arm is no longer upon me. Instantly I miss it, panic, my body suddenly feeling insubstantial, absent.

Am I already dead? When I was a child I would worry about this sort of thing all the time. Mommy, how do you know when you're dead? What if I'm dead already and just don't know it? I gave her a good scare with that one. Lots of "Our Lord Jesus will reunite Grandma and Grandpa in heaven" books appeared around the house after that. Red seven, red seven-ten: the clock alarm starts, an oldies station cranking out Motown fifteen-odd years after the fact. Maybe the cancer is making me go backwards instead of forwards, making my brain devolve back to childhood. Maybe it's time to get up.

Flipping the eggs over easy for Bill and Susie, the coffee brewing in soft gurgles beside me, I suddenly see myself under water. Not in a bathtub, nor in a swimming pool, but in a small, hot-tub-like space. I can feel my cells rearranging beneath the water. It is red water, I think sleepily, lulled by the wet weight of it. Clean water is pouring in through the ducts and new shapes are forming elaborate crystalline structures that can bend radio waves curl sound spin time and I am sleepy the eggs are burning and Susie is calling "Grandma! Your sleeve is on fire!" and then everything is an eggy burning mess.

Only after the dishes are cleaned, the smoky kitchen aired out, Susie and Bill off at the mall in Syracuse for the day, and the house humming along with its electric appliances, do I realize that the red water is my old blood. The ducts need room. The ducts need to get rid of the old blood to make way for the new. Maybe my blood will be dark purple this time, inky like a squid's. I am evolving. I am dying.

I am tired. I station myself at my bathroom window, watching the sparrows settle property disputes in the bare branches of the oak trees. There is a new couple moving in, a fluffy brown sparrow and her more colorful mate. They are noisier than the others, warbling in excited trills over every new twig and leaf they find for the nest. Marriage. You join checking accounts, share a bathroom, raise children, match and mold the rhythms of your life with someone else's. When you're truly married, you forget that this person eating breakfast beside you, rustling the paper as he chews, sighing at all the latest bad news about the Cambodian boat people, is actually a separate person, not just part of your morning breakfast routine. And it's all because of what, sex? The sparrows have flown away, off to look for more nest accessories. Newlyweds, always so extravagant about the nest.

I've been married for thirty-five years. An impossible number, unfathomable, abstract, like the number of new babies born in May in Korea, the cost of wheat in Bengal, the number of angels on the head of a pin. I twist the ring on my finger, trying to anchor my hand to this number.

My wedding ring is gone. I finger the place where the ring should be, my fingertips searching out the familiar feel of the metal band. Instead, a white ring of skin circles my finger, permanently indented from thirty-five years of being encased in gold. When did I last take it off? Probably before one of my millions of baths. I search the vanity, the sink, the corner of the bathtub, all the little nooks where I sometimes leave my ring when I bathe. My mother always told me to remove all jewelry before bathing. "The heat and vapors can ruin precious metals," she intoned with alchemical mystery.

My wedding ring was nothing special: just a plain gold band, no inscription, no decoration. It was my engagement ring that was really snazzy, a full-carat diamond with two half-carats on either side, all of it set in soft white gold. It was a giant diamond princess surrounded by matching half-carat twins, clustered like eager flower girls on either side of her. Bill picked up the ring in Korea during the war, a year before we actually tied the knot. "What a rock!" all the secretaries exclaimed in the office, awed that an old maid like me, twenty-five years old and counting, could snag such a wealthy man. I wore that rock for months, flashing it all over Washington, staving off the advances of the Commerce Secretary and his gang. The gold wedding band was almost an afterthought. I don't even remember where we got it. But over the years, the glamorous diamond engagement ring was retired to my jewelry box, a deposed monarch replaced by the plain ring of gold that I've been twisting around on my finger for thirty-five years.

Of course this was well before the era of the double-ring ceremony, which Mary insisted on having. She fussed incessantly over the engraving of those two matching bands, *Mary and Rod: Peace, Love, Forever.* I thought it was kind of dumb and ungrammatical, but Mary rolled her eyes when I said so at the wedding reception, twisting the band like a talisman.

Myself, I never gave much thought to my own wedding band before, but now it's been circling my finger for so long it's like a separate limb. Without it, I feel severed, like I am that limb, far from my body. My eyes blur, and my whole body caves in at the stomach. Where is my ring?

Sleep curls around me as I lie on the old mat in front of the tub. I dream of my body being stretched around a golden tub full of water. My arms and legs bridge the water, and I cannot move and the cancer cells multiply in the tub.

Jane

The house is veiled in its Saturday morning quiet. Soon her father will awaken, turn on the stereo and quack along to the chorus of disco, disco duck. Then he'll want to enlist Jane to sift flour for Belgian waffles, cooked up in the new stainless steel waffle iron. But now only the refrigerator sings, humming a one-note song all the way down the hall into her bedroom. Jane stands before her dresser. Her hands look through the forest of knick-knacks cluttered across the dresser's top for the tube of glue, the stolen wedding ring, and the blue eye shadow.

Glue, glue, glue, I got glue babe, she sings off-key, sucking in her cheeks and striking a Cher pose for the small, square mirror hung above her dresser. Her hands rove over the lip-gloss, the deck of cards, the dime store superballs covering the dresser's surface. Inside an old wooden jewelry box her dad brought back from some weird woodcarving country behind the Iron Curtain, the little tube waits.

Leah, my Leah, says God. His voice is deep, confident, like the narrator of a documentary on public television. Are you sure you have enough glue?

Jane ignores Him. Her fingers hold the tube tight, squeezing it to near-bursting. Her fingers fish out the bright blue eye shadow she's seen so many times on Mrs. Walkeson's heavy lids, running all the way up to her penciled brows. Jane stares at her own reflection in the mirror. Her lids are so thin in comparison to Mrs. Walkeson's, the blue veins visible beneath the surface. Jane pops the shadow into her jeans pocket, grabbing the gold wedding ring she's buried on her dresser amongst a pile of candy bracelets she bought at Woolworth's, ten for a quarter. Stupid kiddie junk. There is nothing pretty about the pastel sugar-beads, nothing glittery or glamorous in sherbety oranges, limes, pinks, strung together on thin white thread. As Jane pops the ring into her pocket, feeling it nudge against the eye shadow, she scoops up the candy bracelets in her other hand and dumps them in the garbage.

She runs to the vestibule and opens the door of the coat closet and stares into it, like she stares into the refrigerator sometimes, not knowing what she wants, if she's even hungry, just staring at all the food, the jar of pickles with only one pickle left, the bowl of salad from last night's dinner covered in saran wrap, assorted unidentifiable lumps wrapped in aluminum foil. All that food, stored, waiting. She squeezes the tube of glue in her front jeans pocket as she gazes at all the coats hanging together in the coat closet, like strangers waiting together in a line, wordless, motionless. What is she looking for again?

How about a hat. A mikvah hat, God suggests, coughing a little, His voice gravely now, like an old man with a bad cold.

Jane fumbles through the back of the closet, looking for the perfect hat, a mikvah hat for Mrs. Walkeson, something to protect her head from the power of God hovering above, like the yarmulkes men wear in shul when they summon Him up. She digs through the unmatched gloves, the leftover wrapping paper, the chocolate coins left over from Chanukah, ossifying in their gold tinsel paper and yellow mesh bags.

No hats. But in the far reaches of the closet, buried under

old ski sweaters and moth-eaten scarves, she spies a turban, a wool pasha nesting amongst the polyester peasants. Camel-tan, with a large, pinkish rhinestone pasted into the center like a glassy third eye, hovering in the folds of the fine pale wool. The turban is nobody's. Once the turban was owned, left accidentally by a chubby, frizzy-headed blonde lady from Germany who was a colleague of her mother's, a fat historian with nails bitten down to the quick. Now, it lives in the closet, unclaimed, unworn. Jane slowly fingers the turban with one index finger, like she's petting a jittery cat. And then she pops it on her head. The turban makes her head too warm, and it's little itchy right above her ears, but she feels taller, regal, like an Egyptian queen. A mikvah turban. She can feel the pink rhinestone staring down at her like a pupiless eye, unblinking.

With her head encased firmly in the turban, fingers wrapped tight around the silver glue tube, everything is in place.

Leah, what about the mikvah? It's time.

God's voice is pitched higher now, with a distinctly feminine intonation, old-maidish and fussy, a slight wheeze trailing the end of His consonants.

Jane runs across the yard without stopping, through the woods with their leafless trees glistening with melted snow. Everything is rubbed out by the fading night, each specific shape of tree, yard, ground blurring together. The sky says it's going to be another grey day today, the sun smudging dawn across the sky.

She doesn't bother to grab the monorail, for fear of dropping the glue in the dark. God's nagging voice, Leah, Leah, Leah, trails after her, twisting through the spindly trees. Leah, Leah, He drones.

The Walkeson's house is dark, sagging, like it's been waiting on the checkout line for too long at the grocery store. The side door is open; even though it's freezing out, only the screen door is closed. The Walkesons always overheat their house, blasting the heat and opening the windows in the bitter heart of winter. "What a waste. *This* is why there's an energy crisis," Jane's mom says as she zooms the red V.W station wagon out towards Route 81. Today the windows aren't open, but the screen door is letting all the kitchen's heat race out into the yard.

Jane stops, the will to enter melting away. Mrs. Walkeson could be asleep upstairs, bald scalp glistening with sweat as her wig naps on the wicker chair next to the bed. She could be out with Susie, driving her to an early morning soccer practice, nodding in the front seat as Susie recounts her latest triumph beside her. Or she could be in the sauna, mouth parching in the dry heat, each pore opening slowly, like a tightly clenched fist. Or she could be asleep already, nodding off in front of the evening news. That's better: she'll awaken when Jane comes in, make her a cup of cocoa, ask her to stay until *Three's Company* is on, sit her down on the overstuffed couch with Susie and Mr. Walkeson. Jane stands for a long second in front of the screen door, hoping only Mrs. Walkeson is home, curled up on the gold couch with the T.V. on.

She pushes the door open easily, with just a tap. The Walkesons have taken to leaving the kitchen door unlocked, figuring that since the Schwartz's house is the only other home in the Ellis Hills development that has actually been built, there's no need to worry too much about locks and keys and burglars. "They're practically inviting thieves," Jane's mom sniffs whenever she drives by the Walkeson's and see only the screen door protecting their kitchen. Safety, safety first, Jane's mom always says at the Schwartz's bi-yearly fire drills, when they jump out of Jane's second-story bedroom window one at a time. First Jane, then Mom, and finally Dad each perch on the window ledge, then push off, flying down to the soft green lawn. Sometimes, Jane secretly practices on her own. It's not the leap she loves, so much as the moment before, that instant of hesitation, crouched on the ledge, that half-second before she pushes herself into the air. The Walkesons have neither fire drills nor locked doors. Jane stumbles through the kitchen door as if someone is pushing her.

The Walkeson's kitchen is pitch-black. In the dark, it could be any size. Without the lights on, the clutter in the kitchen forms an abstract still-life, a jangle of geometric shapes colliding on the kitchen counter. Without anyone eating the chips from the open bags left on the counter, with no feet walking by the discarded socks in the hall, no hands adding dishes to the pile of dinner plates left on the dining room table, the house is too quiet, too still.

What am I doing here? Jane wonders for a second, wishing she were back in her own kitchen.

Her cheeks burn, shame swirling around her body like a ring of smoke, as if she's already been caught in the act. Breaking and entering: thirty years to life, she hears the judge bark as he bangs on his gavel. She gropes through the kitchen, into the hall vestibule, careful not to touch the walls. In front of their coat closet, she pauses.

What now? She must steal something. No use breaking

and entering if you don't nab the goods. But what can she steal without getting caught? She hesitates in front of the closet, sucking hard on a frizzy curl, imagining the red flash of police lights coming to get her, a detective dusting every surface for fingerprints, footprints, stray hairs.

A coat. They won't think to look for fingerprints on the coats; cloth absorbs the telltale oily lines. The threads will drink in the invisible pressure of a hand, a thumb, a forefinger, the fabric blurring the traces beyond recognition.

The closet is small, crammed with decades of old coats, mateless boots, toddlers' woolen mittens, ungainly mufflers. The brown fur jacket with the white mink collar, hanging primly on a heavy wooden hanger; the green ski jacket that Susie proudly paraded around in school every day last year, well into the spring; the big black down jacket Mr. Walkeson wears to shovel the driveway: all these Jane ignores. The coats are heavy, hard to plough through, their cloth hanging thick and intractable in the closet. At last, an olive sleeve peeks out from behind a plastic yellow rain wrapper. Eureka. A trench coat: perfect for stealthy mikvah-making.

She takes it off its blue wire hanger. It's heavier than it looks, the thick cotton shell lined with olive silk. Too small; she can barely breathe once it's buttoned. She feels like a red pimento stuffed into an olive. But it is a trench coat, and it does have pockets, dozens of pockets: a double pocket inside the left breast for stolen goods, and deep, warm pockets below the waist. With her hands buried in the pockets, she turns away from the closet and faces the basement door. It's cracked open, ready for entry. Wrapped tightly in the coat, Jane slowly make her way to the staircase.

In the dark, the basement could belong to anyone. The

identifying possessions, the detritus of coats, magazines, T.V. guides, and toys scattered around that mark the basement as the Walkesons' are invisible. This could be Jane's own private house, her vast, uninhabited villa. A silent palace without walls, without lights, just dark space opening out infinitely in either direction.

She knocks over a pile of old records at the bottom of the stairs. Chubby Checker? The Beatles? Mozart? In the dark it is irrelevant. Irrelevant, irrelevant, she sings to the night.

Leah, Leah, God calls as she stops in front of the sauna, his voice rich and calm now, no longer wheezing or whining. Leah Leah Leah.

WHAT??? Jane yells back, sick of His chant. WHAT DO YOU WANT? The olive trench coat makes her feel bold, fearless, taller.

Leah, you must make sure the mikvah is really kosher, my dear. Your job is to make it pure, able to withstand even the eldest rebbe's anxious gaze.

She concentrates on the daddy long-legs standing motionless on top of Chubby Checker, focuses all her attention on his ugly gray spider body with its off-pink center. Spiders must have really small brains. She imagines this spider's brain a little pink gob inside the center, running command control for all those legs.

LEAH LEAH LEAH....

Another voice, think of someone else's voice, she commands herself fiercely:

The problem of purity, Mike tells her, hunching over his heavy mahogany desk last Sunday evening as they waited for her mother to come pick her up in the red station wagon, is the problem of knowledge.

Consider the case of the crushed louse.

Seven long days had passed since a woman's period.

Which woman? Jane asks, confused. A very special woman, Mike replies, the half-smile creeping into the corner of his mouth: a hypothetical woman. The woman the rabbis love the best. Jane laughs with Mike, not quite sure what "hypothetical" means.

So we have our hypothetical woman, finally ready to go to the mikvah and rid herself of all impurities. At the mikvah, she examined herself carefully for dirt, blood, ticks, lice, earwax, loose fillings, hangnails. LADIES: PLEASE BE CERTAIN YOU ARE ABSOLUTELY PREPARED FOR MIKVAH: CHECK FOR ANY OF THE FOLLOWING, THE PRESENCE OF WHICH WILL INVALIDATE YOUR MIKVAH, warned the sign in the brightly-lit changing room, whose combination of lockers and floral wallpaper reminds her of the dressing room at a women's gym

The hypothetical woman heeded this advice; after all, she was a careful sort of gal, always checking twice to make sure she'd locked the front door before leaving the house. Spreading her legs wide, opening herself up with thumb and forefinger, she examined every fold, every membrane, every nook and all the crannies. Satisfied that she was spotless, she went to the pre-mikvah shower, the one with the leaky stall, showered twice, showered again to get rid of any infinitesimal organism sneaking around, and proceeded to the mikvah.

Down the stairs to the cool mikvah water she walked. Hands stretched out toward God, touching nothing but the rainwater, she dunked herself under three times.

Kosher,

Kosher,

Kosher, she cried. In three shorts dunks, she was utterly cleansed, purer than vanilla ice cream and twice as sweet.

So hungry for the feel of his skin she was, that night after the long days of separation. As her husband Moishe curled up against her after their love-making ceased, she thought of the baby they might have, certain that today, the purest day of the month, would be the lucky day. Only a perfect child could be conceived from such clean eggs.

The next day she woke up early, head throbbing with pain. As she finished her morning pee, she noticed something black on the toilet paper. Holding it under the light, she realized this was no ordinary speck of dirt, but exactly one-half of the body of a dead bug. "Moishe!" she screamed loudly enough to awaken the neighbors. "Moishe you half-wit! Wake up and tell me what the hell this is." But even before her husband pronounced the word, she knew: it was a louse, or rather, half a louse. An ugly dried-up louse was making itself at home in her vagina on the night she was supposed to be most holy, most pure, most ready for God to enter her and bless her with a baby.

She went to Rabbi Shimi bar Hiyya, the greatest living Talmud scholar in her village, and related the tale. "I was so careful: three showers before, a thorough visual examination after. And I waited seven full days after the last trace of impurity, seven full days," she repeated at least seven times.

The great Rebbe Shimi bar Hiyya conferred with an even greater rebbe in the nearest city of Lodz. The half-louse in question was brought in, examined with the greatest care, its dark half-body dissected and pondered by each rebbe. Some argued that she was only half impure, since after all it was only half a louse that had been found. Rebbe Lodz argued that since the louse had appeared only after the mikvah, her husband's penis must have been the source of the offending creature, thrusting the louse to its ultimate unfortunate destination.

Nonetheless, even if the hypothetical woman herself was not to blame, the fact of the half-louse remained. Would her children be pure? Was her husband contaminated by having intercourse with an impure woman, even though he might himself have introduced the source of her contamination into her body? And despite the fact that she had followed the rules and done a proper mikvah at the proper time in the proper way, was the woman now still truly pure? For though she could have had no knowledge of the tick's presence until after her mikvah, there was no way to determine whether the tick had taken up residence in her vagina before or after the mikvah.

The rebbes debated for centuries over her status, yet no firm conclusions or legal clarifications of the case emerged. But there is no mikvah purgatory. To be judged less than perfectly clean, for one's mikvah to be less than indubitably pure, is to be impure.

Or worse. A body judged neither pure nor impure carries with it the threat of undetectable contamination. It is not simply contaminated, impure, unclean, but the source of impurity. Without a firm opinion in her favor, her status still murky, she became a woman to be feared. It was believed that with just her touch alone she could render young men old, cause instant miscarriages, poison breast milk.

The hypothetical woman was thus disgraced.

Mike's voice trails away. There is silence in the basement

now, though the image of the hypothetical woman lingers. Jane can see her: head bowed, wrapped in long robes, eyes avoiding her husband's. Jane tightens her eyes to summon the image more clearly, as if she's playing the blind man in Blind Man's Bluff. Susie and Jane love the game. Susie prefers to be the one who is chased, while Jane is the chaser, groping about in the dark just as she is now, with only touch, sound, the odd shadow to guide her. The hypothetical woman is weeping now, her nose red and runny.

The smooth wood of the sauna brushes her fingers and the hypothetical woman vanishes. She gropes some more in the dark, index finger searching for, then finding the light switch. The Leah voice is gone, she notices, trying not to think too hard about it so it won't come back.

The sauna lights up as she presses the switch, a dying sun glowing in the dark starless universe of the basement. Jane sets the timer for twenty minutes, the sauna buzzing away as it counts each second. It's time for a plan, she whispers.

Her mikvah must be absolutely blue. Bluer than a freshly-painted swimming pool, bluer than a May sky at dawn, so blue that her eyes can't absorb all the color. Too blue.

Two sources of water are required by law: one still, one running. She will have only the purest spring water, imported from France each week. And fresh rainwater, collected continually in huge buckets outside the mikvah, strained through seven sieves before it reaches the mikvah. Only clean energy will be allowed to heat the water for her mikvah. A special windmill must be made, designed especially to fit the mikvah. A Franklin stove installed, silently heating the pool in the dead of winter. Solar panels built in to the roof above the mikvah, huge glass panels to seize the sun year round.

She tightens the coat around her, ignoring the heat gathering around her in the sauna, overwhelmed. So much to do before the mikvah will be complete.... but what can she do right here, right now?

Get rid of the coat. The mikvah shawl's olive must not compete with the blue. Its fine threads will cover the color, comfort it with its muted tones. She pulls it off, and throws it on the floor, where the dark swallows it up into the murky landscape of the basement.

Two sources of water must run into the mikvah. The Mishnah and Torah have endless qualifications on what water can be used, on the necessity for running water, and the possible exceptions when substitutions such as bottled water can be used.

Again she is overwhelmed. She tries to order her thoughts, make a list in her head, figure out what comes first. First, what will contain all that water, keep it clean, protect it from the dusty benches and hot coals?

It flashes before her: the inflatable blue swimming pool. All last summer Susie and Jane had splashed around in it, playing Marco Polo, sea dolphins, dead man's float. Inflating it was as much fun as swimming in it; they'd take turns hyperventilating into the blue plastic lip. Jane loved the feel as her chest tightened up and the pool stretched its skin, ballooning full of their air. Then one day in late August, Susie decided she was too old for a stupid kiddy pool and demanded that Mrs. Walkeson drive them into Ithaca, to a real Olympic sized YMCA extra-chlorinated pool. Their little kiddie pool was abandoned, left permanently deflated in a corner in the basement.

Now it rests in blue plastic peace on top a pile of snorkeling gear, masks and breathing tubes and flippers piled up like exoskeletons of ancient sea creatures in a natural history museum. Without air, the pool looks insubstantial, like a piece of old clothing, a raincoat perhaps. Jane fishes out the sagging pool from under the snorkeling gear, and starts to hyperventilate.

Everything must be turned off inside the sauna so that the plastic doesn't melt like hot blue lava all over the wood. Jane checks all the buttons on the door to the sauna, making sure there is no hidden secret timer set, no heat lamp booby trapping her plans. Everything must be cool, dry, clean. She grabs an old t-shirt from a pile near the snorkeling gear, and quickly wipes off the dusty sauna.

Kosher. One source of water must be still, one source must come from outside. Running water must mix with still water between the woman's legs. But how can she possibly do this, down here in the basement? Jane thinks a moment: water, water, still and running, where can I get it? The garden hose they'd used to fill the swimming pool last summer will work for the running water, if Jane can remember in which musty corner of the basement it lived. The turban is sitting on her brow now, sliding down towards her eyes as her forehead grows slick with sweat. She pulls a lock of hair out from under it, twisting it around, trying to remember where in the jumble of the basement the hose is hibernating. Before the hair even reaches her throat she remembers: by the old dollhouse, the one she and Susie make into a prison for Barbie when she's bad.

Uncoiling the hose, she drags it to the door of the sauna. Mikvah pool: check. Water source #1: check. Water source #2? Rainwater must be collected. A tube must be run into the mikvah somehow, a tube through which the rainwater can travel after it is collected. For now, tap water will have to do, since neither snow nor rain have fallen in days. A pool of tap water will be immersed in the larger kiddy pool of running water from the hose. But how to inject the still waters into the moving waters? Jane puts a snorkeling mask over her face absent-mindedly, slipping off the turban so she can reach a thick lock of hair. Twisting it between her lips the answer arrives: an inner tube.

For each individual mikvah an inner tube will be filled with still water through the hole meant for blowing it up with air, and then placed in the kiddy pool inside the sauna. The air hole will be opened, flooding the running water with still water. Perfect. Jane snorkels over to the flippers, facemasks, empty aquariums, digging for an inner tube, the bright blue one Susie brought to the swimming pool last August.

Upstairs something creaks. A door opens, perhaps, or the dishwasher grumbles to the sink. It creaks again. A door closes. Or Mrs. Walkeson lumbers from some sleepy corner of the house to make coffee, get the mail, prepare for *General Hospital.*

Listening closely to the noises upstairs, Jane halts her search for the inner tube. She puts on the long green flippers, pulling them tight over her sneakers. They're men's flippers, whale-sized, easy to trip over. With her mask and flippers in place, she makes her way to the stairs, trying not to think of the lie she'll concoct. Something about snorkeling. The creaking is louder now, occurring in irregular, almost syncopated pairs. Something about a vacation, borrowing the snorkel gear for a family trip. Something that will get Mrs. Walkeson to come down and help make the mikvah.

Charlene

What am I?

The question hardens, like sap turning to amber. The inquisitive voice is oddly familiar, yet I can't identify it.

My own voice gives the answer, unwilled:

A gem. An ornament. A carved stone.

I pause, knowing this is not the right answer.

What am I? the voice demands again. It's a little girl's voice, the kind of high-pitched kid's voice that really carries. She answers herself this time:

Gold.

The voice echoes in my ears. Whose voice is this? As I swim toward awake, she repeats herself:

Gold.

And then spells it out, one letter at a time, like a child figuring out a difficult word in a reader:

G-O-L-D

I shift onto my stomach, trying to get the blood moving, trying to force myself out of this murky state, push through towards awake.

What time is it? What day is it? For a few long seconds I am totally disoriented, my own bed a foreign object. The T.V. is on, commercials jabbering about home insurance, Ginzu knives, feminine hygiene. The house is dark. The last thing I remember is falling asleep on the pink flowered sheets in the bedroom, feeling the smooth cotton brush against my face as I fell into a morning nap.

Whose voice was that? Who was asking me such crazy questions?

It was Jane's voice, I realize with a start. Jane, or her dream-ghost double, chirping 'gold' into my slumbering ear. Jane the gold thief. Jane the wedding-ring burglar, invading my dreams.

A greasy smell wafts through the air. Steak gristle, from dinner. It must be late. Or is it early? Maybe the smell is left over, from last night. No, the clock says 4:30. And it's light out.

I lie on my back, trying to regain equilibrium. Need to call Dr. S. Need to stop napping in the middle of the afternoon. Need to get Susie's ballet slippers mended. Need to get my wedding ring back from Jane.

A noise is to be coming from the basement, as if someone is fumbling around in the dark down there. Perhaps an animal is trapped down there, a small raccoon or squirrel, tearing through the old records and Christmas ornaments.

I like the thought of all that junk strewn across the cold basement floor by some marauding creature, the musty old boxes torn to pieces, our ancient Christmas ornaments shattered. When I worked in Washington, my desk was always a disaster, a cluttered uncleanable mess. I used to fantasize about just throwing everything away, cleaning it all off straight into the garbage can until my desk was bare. Now I have a basement twenty times the size of that little Formica desk, and twenty times as messy. Maybe I should hire a team of raccoons to wreck the basement, shred it all into garbage. To break everything to pieces: what raw joy. And then throw it all out, not stopping to extract the valuables from the rubble.

I close my eyes, drifting into the soft folds of the sofa. My body is weightless, as if I am floating an inch above the bed.

144

And my perspective is off: instead of staring down toward my feet from my customary view from the top of my head, I seem to be looking down, as if I were up on the ceiling, perched perhaps on the old ceiling fan. I shake my head and open my eyes wide, staring hard at the room around me. No, I'm looking up at the old-fashioned ceiling fan, with its etched glass details, inherited from Bill's mom; I can't be on it.

And then I am back. The noises in the basement are louder, less random. Could it be a person down there? A burglar? A rodent? The litany begins in my head: need to find out the test results. Need to call Dr. S. Hell, it's Saturday. Dr. S. will be at the eight hole already. He's a devoted golfer, with a "My heart belongs to the eighteenth hole" plaque placed right below his med school diploma on the wall above his desk in the examining room. Such a ruddy-complexioned, healthy fellow, full of hearty laughter and red blood cells. My chest tightens just thinking about all that exercise. I exhale, and start making lists.

Need to clean up the basement. Need to buy a new wig, maybe a brunette this time. Need to get my ring back from Jane. Need to breathe in. out. in.

Jane

Barely alive, barely alive, ha ha ha ha...

The *Mad* magazine record's lyrics repeat in her head as she fills her lungs with air and exhales into the inner tube.

She wraps her lips around the plastic lip, pursed and tight, her head ringing a little more with each inhale, exhale, lungs hurting from the effort. The tube is half-filled, lying like a giant limp donut at her mouth.

Inflation. There's been a lot about inflation on the news, about gas prices, OPEC, and McDonald's all suffering from double-digit inflation. Breath in, push the breath out into the tube. Inflate the tube, deflate the lungs. In, out. And again.

Inside the sauna with the light off, seated on the highest bench with her legs dangling down, she rests the half-filled tube on her lap like an obese baby. She's afraid to turn on the light, afraid it will somehow kick off the heat, melt the plastic, weld it to her lip. A cedary smell emanating from its woody cave, the sauna frames her as she works.

Her flippered feet wiggle as she blows. With the lights off, the sauna is like a closet, a storage space where she might wait quietly until spring, preserved from the moths. She breaths in instead of out, drinking in her own carbon dioxide, feeling the inner tube sag as she sucks up a bit of its air.

Inflation, deflation. You don't hear much about deflation. Just inflation and more inflation. Her lungs fill up with air, and then deposit their garbage into the mouth of the tube. In, out. Her head is getting light, as if it too is filled with helium, carbon dioxide, oxygen. In, out, in.

When she tried to walk in the flippers a moment ago around the basement, she tripped awkwardly, each step a trial, but now, sitting on the sauna bench, legs dangling above the ground, she is a mermaid, swimming her fishy way through a cedar-scented ocean. What does Torah tell us about mermaids? she imagines asking Mike, his thick eyebrows rising in unison as he assesses whether or not she's kidding. What do *you* think the Torah tells us about mermaids? he'd respond, eyebrows still raised, bushy as the winter pelt of a northern animal.

What would the Torah tell us about mermaids? she wonders.

Well, in the beginning the sea was full of them. There were as many different types of mermaids as fish: blue-tailed skinny ones, chubby yellow and green striped ones, little giggly girl mermaids with electric fins that glowed in the dark, and purple eel-like ones who crawled the bottom of the ocean floor.

God played with the mermaids, danced mermaid dances, grew tails himself so that he'd fit right in with them. The mermaids laughed at God—His tail was always too big for His puny body; it formed an unwieldy flippery protuberance, with a few odd feathers sticking out at the end. But He loved His tail, loved racing and diving with the mermaids, loved to watch their heavy breasts bouncing as they dodged Him in a game of tag.

There was one particular mermaid He particularly liked. Her skin was twilight blue, dark and light at once, a color he thought he'd created exclusively for the sky. He called her Shira, "Song," for the melody she hummed as she surfed the waves and chased after fish. He played especially rough whenever Shira was around, wrestling the other mermaids to the bottom of the ocean floor, kicking and grabbing and struggling to win at every game.

I'm showing off for her, God thought one day as He grew an extra tail so that He could be sure to beat the other mermaids at water polo.

I'm falling in love with her, He thought that night back in heaven. He dreamed of making love to her with His feathery tail.

Love, love, love. The word was new to Him, new to the world. Mermaids, after all, laid their eggs in the sand at the bottom of the ocean, and cared little about whoever happened by to fertilize them. And God of course was everything, and nothing. Not nearly specific enough to be in love.

But love was what this was. Oh yes, there could be no doubt about it, God thought as He dove into the ocean the next morning. Love, love, love. He rolled the word around in His head as He swam furiously, looking for Shira.

He soon heard her song at the bottom of the ocean. Shira, light of my life, darkest night of love, oh Shira, He blurted out, unable to shut up, babbling huge bubbles of words all over the bottom of the ocean, disturbing the sleep of the little mermaid-embryos buried in the sand waiting to be fertilized.

But Shira was gone. In the spot where God usually found her was a small pool of fresh water. The salty ocean touched the pool's surface, but did not contaminate it. In the pool God saw His own face and screamed. He forgot all about Shira, thinking only of His own terrible image.

The bubbles grew thicker, God's babble turned into a wail, a tidal wave, a storm, and soon the mermaid embryos were swept from the bottom of the ocean to the surface. When they saw all the dead mermaid embryos floating on top of the ocean, the adult mermaids tore their hair out and turned into fish. God weeped ungodly quantities of tears into the ocean, knowing He would never see His Shira again. The water was brackish, thick with salt.

Nine months passed. One morning, right after dawn, God

148

came down from the heavens and saw a curious sight. Little mermaids were swimming again on the surface of the ocean! As He came closer, He saw that they were not mermaids, but babies, without tails or gills. They were getting tired; some were starting to drown. Shit, God thought. What have I done now?

In a flash God formed dry land, continents, trees, cows, cribs. The strongest of the babies crawled up to the land, and built houses, tribes, beauty parlors.

Since then, every woman must go each month to the mikvah and cleanse the traces of God's tears from her skin. Otherwise, God might remember Shira and throw us all back to the sea.

That's not in Torah, Mike would laugh as she tells him the story in hushed tones. But it's a good story.

Her cheeks burn, imagining his condescending response. She hates condescension. Hates being dismissed. She wiggles her left flipper in anger, feeling the air around her swim away.

Upstairs, the door creaks open. A shaft of light, the outline of a figure with her hands planted on her hips, and the beefy smell of the kitchen all beam down from the top of the stairs into the basement.

Jane's flipper freezes, mid-wiggle.

Dive back.

The words buzz in her head. A soundless voice hums, smooth and silky-soft as a lullaby in her ear.

Leah, Leah my fishy love. Dive back to the sea before you're caught. Dive deep, swim far away. Hurry.

Charlene

I open the basement door. Everything is dark, the stairs descending into pitch black. The noise has stopped. Or perhaps it wasn't ever there?

If I can imagine myself to be a piece of gold, surely I can also hallucinate raccoon noises in the basement. I close the door again, and turn away. I'll wait a minute here, and if I hear the noises again I will...what? Call Bill? Tell him we may have rodents in the basement? Tell him I'm going bonkers? "Okay, Charlene, I can't talk now; we'll deal with this later," he'll say. I can't stand the sound of his voice when he is trying to placate me, all his sweetness suddenly too smooth, a thick solvent. I shake my head, like Jane, insistent, side to side. No, no. No call to Bill. My eyes dilate a moment, then focus. My mother's face.

Her portrait. The wall across from the basement door holds her picture. I haven't really looked at this photo for years. My mother at thirteen. A beautiful, solemn girl, her long blonde hair coiled up in the stiff ringlets fashionable at the time. She hangs across from the basement door, guardian of the basement, in an old sepia portrait framed in heavy tarnished silver. An unusual frame. An unusual gift.

It always seemed like a picture one would hang of someone long dead. "That was my mother as a girl, in '13. She died long ago, you know." But Mother gave it to me herself, a wedding gift.

I thought the picture would make me less uneasy once she was gone, that it would go live in the realm of sentimental trinkets. "Mama's picture," I would tell everyone, a tear forming in my eye. But there is something artificial, something calculated about her picture. Something in the eyes. They gaze out from the soft glow of her sepia face, metal-hard, cold. That stare. It's so hard, so accusatory, like those old carny photos of the man whose eyes seem to follow you.

She stares out from 1909, hands folded in prayer, stiffly facing the photographer in a starched white pinafore. A proper Charleston girl, the daughter of a Sunday school teacher and an industrialist who made his fortune in the bottle trade. For every Coca Cola, a bottle must be made, he would tell everyone with a wry little smile. Tin cans ruined the family business. But there is no sign of ruin in this face. She could be the original Coca Cola girl, a creamy apparition in white with a hint of saucy naughtiness. "Drink Coke!" Her skin is poreless, perfect, her dress crisp and white, everything dainty, refined. Except her eyes, assessing the world icily, finding it wanting.

It was my mother's favorite photograph. "For Charlene—Every happiness forever and more! Love, Mother." An inscription both effusive and vague, scrawled in thick black marker on the back of the photo. Always this...overflowing, hyperbolic love, aimed toward no one in particular.

As I open the door, the blurry world of the basement swallows light, swallows vision, absorbing the stairway into its nondescript grey. I see another universe beneath our brightly-lit living room, housing a whole galaxy of dark blurry shapes. Large, unidentifiable constellations of objects clump across the floor. Another world flourishes down here, a slower world. Except for brief trips to pull out or add to the discarded junk collecting like a layer of fat on the basement floor, we are oblivious to it.

Something makes a crashing sound in the far right corner, over by the sauna. I take a few steps down, not thinking to turn on the light before I make my descent. You must flip the switch at the top of the stairs to illuminate the basement, to reconnect it to the electrified world of 100-watt bulbs and noisy power vacuum cleaners above. Now that I'm halfway down the stairs, it seems easier to wait for my eyes to adjust than to return to the top of the stairs.

"Hello?" I call in a bright loud voice. If Bill were here he would scold me for my lack of caution. "What if Slim Jim got in?" he'd half-joke, using the name he made up for the mysterious thief who kept stealing Mary's bikes back in Washington. In Washington, all the talk was of crime: thieves, criminals, murderers, rapists. Crime, leaping everywhere like an excitable dog, just itching to spring up on its unsuspecting owner. Safety was an icebreaker, a great opener for any conversation: is P.S. 22 still safe? Is your block safe? Your house? Your summer home in Arlington?

But out here in Ellis Hollow I don't believe in crime. Slim Jim and his buddies are credible on the streets of Georgetown, but up here on Hunt Hill, how would he even find us? My own daughter gets lost driving from Ithaca up the twists and narrow broken pavement of Route 79, always managing to miss the turnoff to Ellis Hollow Creek Road, missing again our unmarked lane that curves sharply right and then makes its way up Hunt Hill. Only hunters, local boys tricked out in red coats and air rifles, seem to know the turns that lead up the hill to our house. And they want deer, not diamonds.

Something rustles in the sauna.

"Hello?" I call again. I feel slightly ridiculously. I'm

152

probably talking to a rat.

"Hi Mrs. Walkeson. It's just me."

I can see a masked figure now peeking its head out of the sauna, its brown curls circling out under a snorkeling mask like some strange sea creature's tentacles. It's Jane Schwartz. Is she playing robber again, stealing useless junk from our basement? Cooking up a special recipe? Using the sauna as a microwave?

The light in the sauna goes on, illuminating the rest of the basement with a soft orange glow like a giant night-lite. Jane steps out of the sauna, one hand fingering a curl, straightening it out in her palm.

"You gave me a good scare there, Jane. I thought you were a burglar, trying to steal the sauna or something. What are you doing down there?" As I walk toward the orange sauna, I can see that she is decked out in snorkeling goggles and flippers. Snorkeling in the sauna? "Snorkeling in the sauna?"

"Kind of. Sorry to scare you. I rang the bell, but nobody answered. My parents are gone, and I didn't want to be alone."

I decide to accept this as a reasonable explanation. A turban tops off her snorkeling outfit. It fits: the ensemble doesn't look as ridiculous as it should. Sweating, as though I'm the one getting caught in the act, I open the sauna door and sit on the bench next to Jane. The sauna is off, but it still smells dry and woody, like a long-abandoned campfire.

"You'd better take off those flippers before you break your neck. Mr. Walkeson paid a lot of money for them, and he wouldn't like you traipsing around down here in them."

"Okay."

I can see Jane's cheeks burning red beneath the face mask

as she struggles to pull the flippers off. Her feet glow bare, the skin a warm pink in the orange light. She's humming the theme from *Godspell*, flat and off-key: Day by day by day. I take off my slippers, and line my bare feet up beside hers. My feet are paler, whiter, not absorbing as much of the red light as Jane's. "Have you ever had a pedicure, Jane?"

"A what?" Off come the mask and goggles. In goes a thick frizzy curl, her mouth sucking hard like a nursing kitten. I quickly grab the snorkeling gear and toss it in a pile outside the sauna.

"It's like a manicure, but for your feet. You know, a manicure, like when someone does your nails with polish."

"Oh yeah, I had one of those last summer for Aunt Linda's wedding. I got to wear frosted pink nail polish and a pink polka dot dress. Everyone's nails were painted a different shade of pink."

"Well this is the same thing, but for your toes. Would you like one? I have all the equipment in the bathroom upstairs. I may even have frosted pink polish."

"Okay." In silence, we leave the sauna and make our way in the dark up the stairs.

Upstairs, everything is too bright, too big. Even the vestibule across from the basement door seems enormous, unprotected. I'm relieved when we get inside the bathroom.

Posh Pink Frost. Burgundy Boogie. Trysting Taupe. And that Pat Nixon stand-by: Clear Crystal Rainfall. The names dazzle like hard candies, full of sugar and shine. I introduce them like showgirls in a burlesque, one at a time, reading their full names off the bottles.

Cuticle remover. Scissors. Clipper. Buffer. Clear polish. Q-tips. Cotton balls. Lined up, the pedicure ingredients look surgical, like we're prepping for a major operation. I imagine a nurse solemnly announcing the offending organs to be removed: Liver. Kidney. Tumor. Posh Pink Frost.

"What do we need cotton balls for?" Jane asks as I lay out my wares.

"You'll see."

She sits on the closed toilet seat, feet dangling down. I sit on the floor beneath her, crossing my legs Indian-style. In one hand I take a foot, while in the other I grab the cuticle remover, and begin to press the scaly cuticles back. Her toes are small, the nails a bit long and in-grown. The bottoms of her feet are dirty, but the nails are clean, translucent.

"My goodness! What dirty feet you have. It looks like it's been a while since you've had a proper pedicure."

"Ouch!" Jane wiggles her foot as I press back a particularly thick cuticle on her big toe, a strand of hair winding its way into her mouth. I imagine we're a machine: with each press against the cuticle, another strand of hair will be sucked into her mouth.

"There's nothing worse than nail polish globbed on over a bunch of scaly cuticles. When my daughter Mary was a little girl, she used to get into my nail polish and just paint it on to her toenails, over the cuticles, sometimes painting half the toe in the process. Orange Frost was her favorite color. She looked just like an orange lizard with those scaly painted toes!"

The hair falls from Jane's mouth as she laughs. A drop of spittle sparkles on the end, like a bit of frost on a tree. We don't talk for a few moments; only the sound of my scraping and buffing, against the whir of the dishwasher in the kitchen, breaks the silence.

"So what is cancer?" Jane chirps.

What is cancer? A difficult question to answer. Watching your hair fall out from the chemo? Invisible lumps that only appear on some doctor's x-ray? Sleeping on the gold couch with an overfed cat on your lap, the pink and green pills singing you a soft lullaby all day, the t.v. soap operas chatting along as the hours pass? But these are all just side effects. I think hard.

What on earth is cancer, really? I should know by now. Even though it's been multiplying in my cells for months, I've only felt it second-hand, through the side effects of the treatments aimed at hunting it down, stopping it in its tracks, killing it. Cancer's police. Cancer's stray bullets. Or, better yet: the bullet marks of the cancer-killers. That's what I'm an expert on.

"I don't think they really know, Jane. It's kind of like some of the cells in your body get sick, and start having sick babies, and then these families of sick cells take up all the space in your body, eating up all the room, killing off all the healthy cells." Well, not exactly. My fingers fiddle with the top of Burgundy Boogie.

"Did the cancer eat up all your hair?" Her eyes are bright, with that strange intensity some kids get when they talk about disease. Susie never gets this look, not even when she describes with glee her favorite gross-out monster movie. My Mary's eyes used to fire up at any mention of sickness, death, mutilation. Now Mary's eyes are a dull soft blue. If I had to choose which color they were in the jumbo-sized Crayola box, it would be Periwinkle. Not for the color, but for that blurry, waxy softness.

I finish preparing Jane's nails for the polish, buffing the

tops with an old pink washcloth that clashes with all the gold in the bathroom. "Well, not exactly. It's the chemo that the doctors do to kill the cancer that also killed my hair."

"So if we could get the good cells to kill the bad cells, you wouldn't be sick and they could fix your hair?" Click click goes Jane's brain, whirring away behind those deep-set brown eyes.

"Well, I guess. But no one knows how to do that. Even the doctors are faking it."

Jane laughs. I lightly stroke a thin layer of clear polish onto each toenail.

I hold out the rainbow of nail polishes to her. Greed glints across her brown eyes, frosting them with a glossy metallic sheen. "So, missy, before I let you choose which color you want on your nails, you have to tell me what you were doing in my basement."

Her feet jerk around a bit. "I was just looking at the snorkeling stuff while I waited for you to come home. I thought you were out."

"Now Jane, don't lie to me. I saw you in the sauna. Why did you go in there? You could have waited for me upstairs. I'm not mad; just tell me the truth."

The hair is in the mouth again, twisting around and around the tongue. "Well, I just wanted to try and build you a mikvah." She points to Trysting Taupe. I open the bottle and start to apply as light a coat as possible, like they do in the fancy salons. On her toes, the polish looks pink, not taupe.

"A what?"

"A mikvah. You know, like I told you last time I was over here: it's supposed to cure cancer and stuff. Don't you remember? The Jewish bath thingy."

"I'm still missing something here. What does this Jewish bath thingy have to do with why you were hiding in the porta-sauna in my basement?" Her eyes race around the room, speeding over the gold rug, velvety gold wallpaper, yellow light.

"I just thought I could, you know, build a mikvah thingy in your sauna. See, you're supposed to build it into the ground, but the ground is all frozen outside. But the basement is underground anyway. And you have to have two sources of water and—"

"Now hold your horses." Jane giggles and looks away nervously as I speak. She sucks a piece of hair, an outgrown bang that's hitting her shoulder, back into her mouth. "You can't just go building mikvah churches in people's basements without their permission! Mr. Walkeson wouldn't like it very much if he came home to take a sauna and found a bunch of Jewish cancer gunk in there."

Jane is giving me that sullen look now. I can feel the little muscles where sullenness is stored on my own cheeks. "A mikvah isn't a *church*, Mrs. Walkeson. Jews don't have churches; we got synagogues. And it's not a synagogue, either. It's a bath." Her mouth is tight and prim, bunched up into a pissed-off bud. She is the basement rat after all, nibbling up my old records, empty dollhouses, abandoned roller skates. All she lacks is a tail.

"And a sauna is a sauna, not a bath or temple or mikvah. Really, Jane, you should know better than breaking into someone's basement! I don't think your mom would like this mikvah bath idea very much, especially if she heard about the sauna break-in."

Jane shrivels up her nose at the mention of her mother and makes a face. A hair gets sucked up into the nervous smiling mouth like a piece of spaghetti. The mouth gnashes on it a bit, chewing, tense. "So are you going to tell her? And do I still get the rest of my—what did you call it—pedi, pedi-something?"

"No I won't tell and yes you get the pedicure. Be a little patient, missy; I can't put another coat of polish on until once the first one is completely dry. And I'll tell you what: we can build a mikvah, but not today. Maybe on Monday, after my doctor's appointment. Susie will be at soccer and your mom wanted me to watch you after school that day, anyway, since she's got an appointment. But," I hold up the wand of Burgundy Boogie, pointing toward Jane like a fairytale magic godmother, "you have to promise that the mikvah won't leave a mess in the sauna. And you have to promise to clean it all up afterwards. Last time you were over and we made licorice hot chocolate, I had to throw away the burnt pan you left. You got the chocolate, but all *I* got was a burned pan!"

Jane laughs, a lock of hair blowing out of her mouth. "Okay, but don't forget. Monday is our mikvah day."

We don't talk as I apply another coat of polish, Burgundy Boogie this time, to each toe. Like plump old ladies with pink hair, fresh from the beauty salon, the toes peek out from under their polished heads.

When I'm finished, I file the tops of her toenails, buffing them with a cloth. "Voila!" I declare. My back is tight, all the muscles crunched together like a fist from kneeling for too long. I pull the cotton balls out from between her toes, and pile them beside her. We both stand up.

Jane grins as she examines my handiwork upon her toes. A sweet, dimpled smile graces her face, her small teeth peeking out between her thick lips like well-polished grains of rice. She wiggles her toes delicately, grinning first down at them and then up at me. I notice her mouth is free of hair.

"Jane, you have a lovely smile. When you don't suck that darn hair of yours, I can see what a terrific face you have."

Her smile falls away, a scowl replacing it. Even though she's not sucking her hair, her mouth moves, teeth grinding over an imaginary lock of bangs. She glares at me fiercely. "Yeah. Well, I should go home now. So are we on for the mikvah, Mrs. Walkeson?"

"You bet. Monday afternoon, before I pick up Susie from soccer, around, oh, four. But you have to help me clean up from the pedicure now."

Together we re-cap the polishes, throw away the cotton balls, and mop the floor with paper towels. We wash our hands in the bathroom sink, the cool water and white slip of soap carrying away the traces of nail polish remover, old skin, floor wax. The bathroom is clean again.

As I watch Jane dry her hands on a yellow bath towel, I notice how uneven her pinky nails are. They pitch up at the sides, lurch down at the center, and then go up again at the other side like a ridge of mountains formed by angry glaciers. "One more thing," I tell her. "Let's do a manicure before the mikvah on Monday. Your fingernails are a mess. We'll make them nice and smooth, just like your toenails."

She nods, her ponytail bobbing up and down. And she scuttles away, a well-pedicured crab sliding sideways out the kitchen door.

It's only after she's left and I'm nested at my porthole

window looking out into the bare trees that I remember my gold ring. My fingers are reaching for the familiar band to twist as I stare out. Instead, they find a slender ring of white flesh.

Jane, you thief, I think as I touch the circle where the gold is gone.

CHAPTER 7:
SUNDAY

Jane

The blood is blood.

Her mother had explained it all before, many times: it's just menstrual fluid, skin cells and mucus, not 'blood' really; there's only a drop or two of actual blood in it. A day or two beforehand, you'll feel it coming. Below your tummy, your uterus will swell up, and you'll feel a little cramp like a stomachache, except lower down. But there's not a lot of blood involved: just a teaspoon or two. It's just the lining of your uterus shedding, like a snake losing its old skin. Or like when we replace the heavy grey winter flannel sheets with light blue cotton sheets in our beds each spring. It's not really "blood"; that's an old-fashioned myth.

But the blood is blood. There it is in cold blood, on her sheets, first thing in the morning. Blood streaking everything. Bright crocus red, splashing her thighs, sticking to the sheets.

Jane woke up early, with her hand pressed between her thighs, feeling something wet on her fingers. For a moment, she wondered whether she'd peed in the bed. As she pulled the blankets and sheets off, she saw the blood, splotching red on her hand. On the sheets. Staining into the mattress.

She had thought it would be thicker, more like snot or

glue. But it trickles, runny and thin like a half-healed cut. And there are no cramps, no swelling, no "PMS" like in the Midol commercial. Just blood. Blood, smeared up her thighs. On the sheets. On her fingers.

"Gallons of it," she insists, showing her mother the sheets a minute later.

"Jane, must you always exaggerate? The experts say an average woman only expels about a quarter of a cup of fluid per menstrual cycle, and of that, only a teaspoon full or so is actual blood."

Jane imagines a line of chubby women circling the earth, each holding a measuring cup filled exactly a quarter of the way up.

"Well it sure looks like blood to me!" Jane blusters as she pulls the stained sheets off her bed. The blood is dark, an eggplanty purple against the powder blue of the flannel sheets.

"It's just a little menstrual fluid. I'll get you some pads, fresh underwear, and a Midol. The sheets can be bleached." Her mother starts stripping the bed, ignoring the red stain on the mattress.

"I don't need any Midol, and I already have pads in my bathroom, remember? Just let me take care of it."

But the sheets are already off. Her mother folds them up into little squares as if she's packing them away for a trip. An awkward smile flickers at the sides of her mother's mouth, and then she piles up the neatly folded squares of sheet and leaves, carefully closing the door behind her.

The blood-red blood. Jane examines the stain left on the mattress, spread like a child's finger-painting in a messy mass across the fabric. First it's dark, an outrageously shit-colored brown. Then towards the center, the stain changes to scarlet. A rainbow of blood.

And the smell! Vinegary. Slightly rancid, like salad dressing kept too long in the sun. No one had mentioned the smell in those "A Girl's Special Time" films in health class. She lies on her back on the sheetless bed, feeling the blood trickling its way down her leg, inhaling the loud stink of it.

The blue cover of Rabbi Loewe's treatise on *The Jewish Path in Sex, Love, and Marriage* peeks out from under her pillow. Jane flips herself onto her stomach, and pulls him out.

Page 33: Section One: *Niddah*. Impurity, Followed by Section Two: Proper Behavior for the Niddeh. A *niddeh*, they call her, turning the name of the law into her proper name. An "impure one." The Niddeh, the law says, must avoid all contact with her husband during her period and for seven days after. Until she is absolutely clean, her underwear spotless, her sheets unstained blue like the summer sky, she is Niddeh, impure in state and, Niddah, the impure one, noun and adjective at once. Double trouble. Jane fingers the stain again, tracing its outline upon the light blue mattress, a throbbing pain making its way from her stomach to her thighs. Nobody ever mentioned leg cramps. She flips the page, looking for better news.

Page 34: Female Impurity and Mikvah. A woman must not enter the mikvah during her time of impurity and for seven days hence, Rabbi Loewe reports. She is in an impure state, and must scrupulously avoid contact with men and any object which a man may also touch. And then a list, of all the different cases of female impurity, hundreds of them, indexed by the talmudic and midrashic reference numbers for all the millions of rabbis' trillions of commentaries. *Impurity,*

Major Types: Impurity of items on which a woman lay before discovering menstrual blood: Niddah 5b-6a. Impurity of items on which a woman lay before discovering a menstrual bloodstain: Niddah 6a.

Her eyes blur as she tries to read them all. It's so confusing. How can she be responsible for stuff she lay on last night, before she even knew she was bleeding? Jane traces around the edges of the stain on the sheet, outlining it over and over with her index finger. She reads more:

Impurity of Sitting on an Item - Moshav. Impurity Communicated by riding on a horse is Communicated via the front legs, on a donkey via the rear legs: Shabbat 93b.

She can already imagine Mike's interrogation on this one: Could impurity be communicated by the front seat or the back seat of a Volkswagen? If it had four-wheel or two-wheel drive? If she bled straight through the seat, into the foam cushions underneath, drenching the engine, gas tank, chassis? There are so many questions she could ask him. Is a chassis kosher? Why is "Communicated" capitalized?

The list goes on:

Contracting Impurity. Impurity of a man who slept with a woman shortly before she discovered blood: Niddah 6a, 14a. Impurity of a man who slept with a woman shortly before she discovered a bloodstain: Niddah 6a, 14a, 15a. Impurity of a man who slept with a woman shortly after she discovered a bloodstain: Niddah 14a, 15a

Laws, laws, laws. Who on earth could possibly remember them all? Jane closes the tome, dipping a corner of the blue cover into the blood on the mattress. It doesn't leave a stain.

"Jane?" her mother calls. "Are you in there, Jane? I'm stopping at the pharmacy before I go to work. Do you need anything for your, you know, menstruation?" She jingles the car keys for emphasis.

"No, I'm fine. Do I have to go to shul? I'm getting really bad cramps now." Only once the words slip out does she realize she will not, cannot, absolutely won't go to shul. No Mike today. No way.

A sigh whistles from the kitchen. "Ufff. Janie, it's not a disease. I really don't want you thinking of your period as a sickness."

"I *know*, Mom. But I really have cramps!" Jane shouts.

Another whistling sigh, an even longer one this time, flies out of the kitchen. "Honey, you can't miss school every time you get your period. I get my period every month, and I still teach classes, do my research, go on trips, even jog. You really shouldn't let it stop you from..."

Jane's hands cover up her ears like earmuffs, making everything warm and silent. SHUT UP! SHUT UP SHUT UP! she mouths at the door. The sigh ufffs out again. Finally the garage door opens and the v.w. station wagon wheezes out. Jane sits on the sheetless bed, examining the stain, its rainbow of reds.

Her index finger outlines the spot on the mattress, tracing the color from brown to brick and back to brown again. She rubs it hard with her palm, spitting on it to moisten it. The spot darkens. It's still bright red: a sort of cherry red-black. She pulls down her pants, and dips a finger underneath her underpants. It comes out tipped with blood, wet and bright orange. This is the test.

How many days left until she can do the mikvah? How many days until her hand comes out clean, until no specks of blood or this weird black sludgy stuff stain show on her panties? How to keep track? It has to be seven days, exactly, from the time her hand comes clean until she can dunk. She will have to test every day.

She pulls her pants up, wiping her finger on the mattress. From under her pillow, she takes out the blue test book she's swiped from her mother.

From the mess of superballs, stolen eye shadows, and bubble gum wrappers on her bureau, she picks out three pens. Frowning down at a new, clean page with thin blue lines that run across it, she makes a plan. She will number each red day with a red pen; each clean day with a blue pen. She will write down the days of the week and put a check in red next to the red days and a check in blue next the blue days. Checks and balances, like in government. Today, Monday, March 3rd, is red.

Leaning on the messy bureau, she writes down the date with her red pen on the first blue line at the top of the page, and starts to make a red check beside it. But instead, she scribbles in dense, short marks, covering the whole page until it is a bright red square.

Then, in thick black ink that bleeds a little into the red background as she presses down on the pen, she writes:

NIDDAH

and underneath in pencil:

DAY 1.
and underneath that:
As of 8 a.m. this morning, I am a niddeh.

A niddeh: an impure one. A noun. The rebbes sometimes refer to her as "*the* niddah," as if there's only one.

A good question for Mike: why do they act like there's only one? It's never the niddehs, just a solo niddah. Is it the same in Hebrew?

She will ask him tonight. She will contaminate the wicker and leather seats of his house, the bright yellow kitchen, the chamomile tea bags, his wife's bathrobe hanging by the shower. Spread her skin cells across the carpets, floors, beds. Drip red through the hallways, like a sunset spreading fire through each room. Turn everything impure, everything niddah, mark it red, make it up like a teacher's red pen on paper.

The black ink bleeds into the red. She is niddeh: her touch will turn gold to shit. As it is written: from the first day of her period until there is no trace of it on her panties, she is niddah, and all she touches is niddah, too. This polo shirt, those jeans: all niddah, she thinks as she dresses. All mine.

And then? Page 36: *The White Period.* For seven days after the last trace of her period disappears, she enters the White Period, still contaminated, the White Queen. Only after seven days and seven full nights pass, above and beyond the days of her period, can she enter the mikvah and purify herself.

Out in the kitchen her father is singing "I am woman hear me roar, and I do not need to snore," -oar rhymes tumbling out in quick succession.

As if it's an afterthought, she shoves in a pad from the pile her mom left on the bed, pushing it inside her underpants before she zips up.

"Jane, I'm leaving. If we don't go now, I'm gonna be late. Mom said you should go to Mike's even though you're...

feeling sick." His voice booms loud, reaching behind her closed bedroom door.

"All right already, I'm *coming*. You don't have to shout. I'm not deaf, you know." She grabs Rabbi Loewe and her notebook, suddenly looking forward to sitting across from Mike, being grilled on niddeh when he doesn't even suspect she's niddah, right then and there.

"Don't get snippy with me, Janie. And get your butt out here. 'Ready' means in the car."

She feels the blood flowing a bit now as she stands up, trickling between her legs. It's as if the lower half of her body has suddenly come into focus: legs, butt, crotch, stomach all becoming distinct, clarified by the blood running through them.

Charlene

I know how to reach this sound. I close my eyes, lean back in the filled tub, and let the water cover me completely. Submerged beneath the bath water's surface, I listen.

Shhh. This is the voice of water, the sound of hydrogen ionizing with a pair of oxygen molecules. Stretched out at the bottom of the bathtub, my hands gripping the sides to resist flotation, to keep me here beneath the water's surface, I try to hold my breath another second so I can hear that sound longer.

RRRR

RRRR a harsh noise breaks through from above the

water's humming surface.

RRRRRing, I bring my head up, ears still filled up with water, and pull myself out of the tub. Splashing up the bathroom, slipping a bit in the hallway as I make my way into the chilly morning, grabbing the comforter off the bed to cover my wet body as I run, I race toward the phone.

"Mrs. Walkeson, please?"

"Speaking." His voice sounds far away. The water, the water in my ear, I think: it's blunting everything. I pull the green down comforter off the bed and wrap it around my wet body. I look like a triangular tree, a Christmas tree with my head as the star at the top.

"Dr. Samuelson here. Some confusing news."

It must be confusing, indeed, if Dr. S. is calling me on a Sunday afternoon.

"While the overall quantity of cancerous cells has been reduced, presumably due to the chemo, your blood work shows that there is some evidence that the cancer has traveled to your kidneys, causing the possibility of major dysfunction." As usual, he talks in condensed paragraphs, a sort of summary-speak I remember overhearing from Washington lawyers who billed by the minute. "I'm afraid this means we've crossed over from stage I to stage II cancer, and we'll need to reassess our treatment options. Can you come in on Monday?"

Crossed over. I can't concentrate on his words: crossed, crossed over, kriss-kross.

My mouth spits out the correct responses: "Okay Doctor, thank you for calling, can you tell me exactly what the numbers are, what this means, how exactly my kidneys might be affected, what my chances are looking like?" But my ears are closing even as the words pour out.

It's the noise from the bath, I think idiotically. My ears are stuffed with it, too filled to take in any more sound. Perhaps it's those drops of bath water stuck in them, absorbing all the words. I shake like a wet dog, trying to clear my ears. Listen to the Doctor, my mother would always say. My ears ache with listening, my eardrums funneling his words—to where? Where do sound waves go once they're heard? My mind is running ahead of his voice. Concentrate, concentrate. Take it one word at a time. Start with "crossed."

The cancer has crossed. For some reason, that's all I can hold on to. I try to imagine the cancer crossing, from lymph to liver, from Stage I to Stage II, from "cancer may be eradicated with early intervention" to "cancer likely to continue spreading." Instead, as I hang up the phone, I think of my crossed toes, clinging placidly together. I give them a wiggle.

"Better crossed toes than crossed eyes," my mother always said when I'd wiggle them before her. I liked them crossed, stuck in a perpetual embrace, the little piggy who stayed home folded tight against his neighbor.

We had to journey downtown to Linman Bros. each September to measure my feet for special orthopedic shoes. I'd dutifully flatten my foot against Mr. Linman's heavy metal foot-measurer, inhaling the scent of his lemon aftershave. Linman Bros. was a solemn place, a serious store with wood paneling and wine-red carpeting, quiet as a Methodist church on Monday morning. Mr. Linman spoke in a hushed voice, pondering each foot with a heavy sigh as he measured it. "Two crosses. Hmmf. Dearie me. Quite unusual," he'd inevitably whisper. There was no brother at

Linman Bros.; it was just Mr. Linman and hundreds of made-to-order orthopedic shoes.

Sample shoes rotated around in the window like frosted cakes in a pastry shop, mounted on pedestals draped in velvet. There were a wide range of styles on display, from elegant lady's navy blue pumps to shiny pink ballerina slippers with boxed toes, but they were not for me. They were not orthopedic. Orthopedic shoes for girls came in only one style: plain black leather flats with thick laces all the way up to the ankle, "for extra support," as Mr. Linman whispered each time as he fitted me. I don't know how the extra ankle support was supposed to uncross my toes. You didn't ask questions at Linman Bros.

I didn't mind my special, ugly shoes. I liked going downtown with my mother, not once but twice: first for the fitting, and then again to pick them up and make sure they fit. My sister Meredith had no crossed toes, so she got regular brown-and-white saddle shoes from the Sear's catalog, and only occasionally got to come along for the big excursion to Linman Bros. Each trip down to Linman Bros. was topped with ice cream sodas at Hanson's around the corner. I always got a Brown Cow, with one scoop of French vanilla ice cream floating in a sparkling root beer sea.

I liked the black polish, Mr. Linman's whisper, the Brown Cow. I even liked getting my foot measured, feeling Mr. Linman's tape measure moving across the length, width, and in-step, watching his bald white head bobbing up and down. "Let's have a look at those toes," he'd say before he finished. And each time he'd glare down at my crossed toes, still crossed, still hugging tight together, September after September.

172

They never did uncross, despite all that extra ankle support. Star-crossed lovers they remained. All those years of crossing has made them grow closer together, so they fit like jigsaw puzzle pieces, one bulging fat where the other one is thin. By the time I was thirteen, we were too poor to afford orthopedics, so I started getting the same saddle shoes as Meredith, delivered direct from Sears to our doorway.

I look down at my feet, peeking out from under the green comforter. Yes, my toes are still crossed, still stuck on each other. I bend down and pull them gently apart, one at a time, feeling them twinge at the root as they separate for a second, and then fall back together, incorrigible mutants.

Jane, however, has perfect feet. Each toe lines up beside the next, untwisted. The nails themselves are free of dirt, deformity, or that awful scaliness that Susie seems to have inherited from Mary. Whenever I pedicure Susie, I think of the claws of my mother's bathtub. But when I polish Jane's toenails, I think of vegetables, fresh carrots or celery stalks stacked beside one another at the grocer's. What well-arranged feet.

I look down at my own feet again. They look fine, really; the skin is a bit dry around the heels, but otherwise they look young, unspotted by those brown age spots dotting my hands. Has the cancer crossed over into my toes? Into the in-between spaces where our ancestors once had webs? Is lymphoma building waterways around my ankles, down into my big toe, across the inside arches?

Only my mother would remember about the crossed toes. She's gone, I'll be gone, these silly toes of mine will be gone, and no one will remember. In family photos, when my great-granddaughters peer at my image, they'll see no toes.

When my sister's children's children's children tell stories about me, they won't know about the toes. How they chafed against each other. Which crossed over which.

I wander back into the bathroom. My ears have unplugged. The water trapped inside must have somehow mysteriously worked its way out of the canals, into the ether.

The water in the bathtub has also drained out, leaving a yellow ring on the sides. I sit on the side of the tub, naked, a bit chilly. Dangling my feet beneath the faucet, I turn on the hot water, full force. The water gurgles as it hits my feet, turning the flesh across the top of my feet a bright, pepperminty pink. I keep the drain open, so the water trickles down after it coats my feet, dribbling between my toes. I feel like a figure in a fountain, one of those little naked boy statues you see in Europe, the water dripping out of him like he's peeing. Except it's my toes the water runs through, passing through me on its way to drain, trickling over and between all ten toes, its volume never increasing, never decreasing. I watch it, mesmerized, immobile as any fountain statue. Cancer, crossed toes, calls from the doctor: everything recedes as I watch the water swirls down the drain.

I want my ring back, I think out of nowhere. Somehow I keep forgetting about it, only remembering at these odd moments when Jane's not around. Jane can have her mikvah down in the porta-sauna, but I need my ring.

174

Jane

No answer.

She waits at the door, finger poised over the bell, not sure whether or not to ring again. The house is quiet, no light animating its stern white colonial flatboards, but then again, Mike and Shoshanna often leave the lights off, trying their best to help President Carter with his wear-extra-sweaters-and-turn-your-thermostat-down campaign.

Jane's mom loves Jimmy Carter, his Southern drawl, goofy toothy smile, his tough talk about the energy shortage. Her mom even bought her dad a tightly-knit brown and white argyle sweater just like the one the President wore on his last televised fireside chat. Her dad says Carter's a hick, a peanut-farming idiot who doesn't understand the first thing about science. But he wears the sweater.

Mike never wears sweaters. Mike doesn't seem to get cold, even though he only wears a plain white oxford cloth shirt, blue jeans, black yarmulke. Always he sweats, even outdoors, even in the frigid Ithaca spring.

Her feet are freezing, turning blue in their navy blue sneakers. It's a cold afternoon, colorless, the sky a headachy gray going black, even though it's only a little after four. Could he have forgotten about their appointment? Or maybe thought that she had forgotten, since she didn't show up on Wednesday, and she's so late today? Damn. Damn, damn, damn. She peers through the front window, her feet chilled to the ankles, and presses the doorbell again, one Mississippi, two Mississippi, three, until she hears footsteps padding down the hall. Slow steps. Deliberate steps. Every movement he makes is always so deliberate, considered.

They make their way together silently through the dark house to the study. He turns on the hall lights as they go, not breaking the silence. In his study it is especially dark. Too dark even to play Blind Man's Bluff. He doesn't turn the light on, so she stumbles a bit as she finds her seat. The ceiling seems to hang particularly low today, reaching down toward the floor. She stares up at it, not meeting his gaze. It's stucco, with little bumpy pointy things poking out. "So what do you think of all this mikvah mishegas?" he begins.

"I don't know."

"What do you mean, 'I dunno?' Surely you have one thought, however small, about something as kinky as mikvah!" His mouth is twisting hard at the side, eyes pulling hers down from the ceiling. She doesn't meet his gaze. If she were the size of an ant the ceiling would be a whole universe, the bumps mountains, the points dangerous precipices

"I don't know," she repeats. "I mean, it just seems weird that there's so much law about it and it doesn't even really exist anymore, except among the real religious crazies in Brooklyn or Israel or something."

He smiles. A good answer. "That's true, though of course Brooklyn and Israel are hardly the same place. But more importantly, there are lots of important rituals that gradually lost their relevance. Come on, Jane, you've read enough Torah to understand how central animal sacrifice was. It hasn't been practiced since sometime around the destruction of the second temple in—"

"Seventy A. C. E."

"Good. Or look at all those endless fucking laws monitoring polygamy. Today, supposedly, only monogamy is kosher. But almost every bit of Talmud concerned with t'annit niddeh or family planning or fucking is also about how to keep all your wives happy. Look at Abraham. Look at Saul. Polygamists, all of them. But polygamy's not the point. The point is," he exhales sharply, the 's' whistling out, his thick mustache wobbling a bit like a fake Halloween paste-on, "The point is, and most rabbis won't admit, but every generation of Jews must figure out what's worth preserving, what's not. Not individually, but collectively, through Mishnah, through Torah study, through debate, through their actions." He's ranting now, the litany pouring through his mouth without pauses, a stream of words singing out, playing loud long chords against her eardrum. "Polygamy or monogamy. Mikvah or no mikvah. The law is an effect of the conversation, and just as contentious and mutable."

Contentious. She'll have to look that one up. Mutable: changeable. Or is it also like 'mute,' as in deaf and? It could mean both at the same time: changeable and deaf. Like Mrs. Walkeson's cancer, mutating, changing all the time, turning a deaf ear to chemo.

He's still talking about law, the concept of it, whether we still need it, what happens when there is none. Jane nods along, practicing being mute.

"You're a quiet one today. Did you really do all the reading?" he suddenly asks, interrupting his own train of thought, furrowing his thick brows together and inclining his head in toward hers like they are two old birds.

"Huh? Uh, yeah."

"Okay then. What do you think you'll want to do with this mikvah business when the time comes?"

When the time comes. Which time? The pad between her

legs is scratching her thighs. "You mean–'

"When you get married. Will this seem at all relevant? This mikvah business, or is it sexist shit, stupid crap made up by old men who think women's cunts are dirty?"

He looks closely at her, searching for signs of shock. She holds her face still, like it's a plate filled with fragile knick-knacks that must not be broken. Don't move, she commands her muscles. Don't breathe too hard. Don't give away the secret. Don't let him know about Mrs. Walkeson and the mikvah, no matter what he asks. Don't tell about Leah. Don't talk about the pedicures. Stay calm. Mute.

"I don't know," she says, staring straight into his black eyes.

"'I don't know?'" he falsettos back at her, his gaze like a sharp slap across the face. The room falls still. He might hit her. He might ask for evidence. He might cry. He holds his stare, her eyes glassing over with tears.

And then he gets up from his seat, looks at his watch, grunts in disinterest. "Well, think about that for next time, and come up with a more interesting answer than 'I don't know.' And read Rashi 23:1. And take the hair out of your mouth." He turns away, pulls a book randomly off the shelf of millions and trillions of Hebrew books whose titles she can barely read, and he starts to read. This is the cue: she should leave the study now.

She walks through the house towards the front door, to wait alone until her father drives up to take her back home. In the foyer, a weak overhead light turns everything a grayish pink as the blood trickles down her thighs and tears spill into her mouth and mix with the taste of her unwashed hair.

178

Charlene

I press hard. My forefinger presses into the thin flesh of my underarm, hoping to feel a lump, a node, a tangible sign. I want to finger the cells beneath, trace their trade routes as they travel underneath my skin.

Blood, piss, saliva: sure, I'd thought of them plenty, each with its intricate architecture of canals and rivers winding through my body. But the lymph system? I couldn't picture it. I tried to read up on it, learn everything I could, become an expert on all things lymphatic. Left over from that era of my home-spun expertise is a single brochure.

"You and Your Lymphoma," reads the title, done up in cheery pink lettering on creamy off-white paper. I keep it here on the toilet seat with a couple of old *New Republics* and *Redbooks*. The nurse handed it to me after the diagnosis six months ago. I memorized the pamphlet, then went to the big white marble public library in downtown Ithaca to look up all the original sources cited in the bibliography in the back, poured over endless articles written in tiny print in colorless medical journals. But now I just want to feel a single sign of it, grab the bull by its proverbial horns, touch a lump, a bump, a growth; even the slightest protrusion would do.

But I feel nothing. After all, lymphs are not fleshy tumors sprouting like wild mushrooms under my skin. 'Lymph' is just a fluid, a colorless watery liquid that carries along the white blood cells, storing them in bean-shaped little organs called "lymph nodes." These I had heard of: lymph nodes, famous for swelling beneath the neck when a child breaks out in fever. Mary never had any such swelling, but I remember hearing the other mothers talk about it. From what I gleaned from my research, lymph nodes are normally like small clinics buried inside the body, manufacturing armies of white cells to take on the barrage of diseases parading through the body. They are good, honest doctors, pumping out white blood cells, killing bacteria, fighting crime. But too much of a good thing, as my mother would say, not finishing the sentence...

I poke harder, deeper into my underarm, against the uneven tufts of hairs. I haven't bothered to shave in this region since the chemo.

Lymphoma makes all the white cells traveling along the lymphatic system grow abnormally, Dr. S. told me when my results came back this morning. "What do you mean, 'abnormally?'" I asked, somehow not expecting Dr. Samuelson to be able to define what exactly this meant. But he did. They divide too rapidly, growing wild, without order or control. Too much tissue is formed. Tumors grow. They can be individually eradicated. But the abnormal growth can't be stopped. His sentences got short and concrete, carefully parsed, carefully pared down to the cold facts, just the facts, ma'am.

I pinch my underarm skin with my thumb and index finger, grasping the thin skin around one long, straggly hair, as if I could squeeze a tumor out of the follicle like a tick. But they are travelers, these tumors, moving invisibly into the inner organs: first the liver, then the spleen, then sometimes even, incredibly, into the bone itself. Anywhere the lymph system goes, the lymphoma travels, scattering cancerous tumors across the body, like Johnny Appleseed gone haywire. In a normal body, white blood cells are a necessity, manufactured to kill bacteria and other invading organisms. But when you have lymphoma, the white cells take over, like a too-zealous army invading its home country, raping and looting its own civilians. Too few white cells, and your body is defenseless against foreign invasion; too many, and it invades itself.

I ponder this a second, still holding on to the flesh I've pinched. What a scam! It's kind of like abnormal profit. A profit, after all, exists only when, after you pay your suppliers, capital expenses, your workers, give management a raise, pay off any outstanding debt, give the government its share of taxes, you still have something left over. Every company plans for a certain amount of profit, which itself is a form of excess; anything over that predicted excess is an abnormal profit. Now, your average CEO lives for profit, abnormal or otherwise. He loves to hear the word, rolls it over and over on his tongue, "profit." He gives his accountant an instant raise when he hears, "We have an abnormal profit here. You're in the black!"

Companies tend to expand too quickly when they see a profit, open too many new plants, offices, factories. Or, worse, they invest in the market, always a dicey, chancy game. They get cocky. They over-invest, over-extend, over-develop. Soon they are investing more than just the excess profit, leading to debits, deficits, unsold products, lost jobs, bankruptcy.

But the secret about profit, even the most abnormal sort, is that it ultimately is simply a number. It can be turned into more numbers, its force used for capital, equipment, stock, or it can be squandered, overextended, risked, reduced to debt. Then you're back in the red again, everything a minus, the numbers all less than zero. The numbers reverse so easily.

181

I live for numbers. They always teased me about my penchant for accounting. "All those numbers; however do you keep track of them all?" my mother would ask when I was studying cost accounting late into the night in college, even though it was she who had suggested accounting as a practical course of study for an unmarried woman. "You've got great legs, for an accountant!" Bill would tease when we first started dating. Bean counters, number nerds, tax spooks: I've heard it all. Everyone views accounting as drudge work. The OMB boys in Washington called us the "budget burglars."

But accounting is a subtle art. Good accountancy is like drawing a portrait. You look at the heart of a transaction, and out of the mess of credits and debits and debts, you sketch a face. Your job is to paint a coherent picture, tell the story through a single set of numbers. You must observe each number carefully, catch it precisely in your account. Drawing in numbers, you must use a limited vocabulary to show the face. It is not so much a question of counting, but piecing together a convincing account of a given set of exchanges. And I was the best at it: at tracking, watching, observing, noticing. I drew good portraits.

When I was a girl, I'd try to figure out what kind of number each person was. It was a strange power, to squint at my mother and see an elegantly curved 9, to see my sister as a 5, a prime number indeed, divisible only by herself.

Jane is also a prime number. A 7, skinny and awkward, but with a sort of symmetry nonetheless. Mary, on the other hand, is more like a single-digit even number. An 8: so evenly formed, top and bottom matching. Boring. And Susie? I don't think she's a number at all. A letter, maybe, a big, carefully drawn "S." But not a number.

I pinch beneath my arm again, just once, fast. Time to get cracking. Need to go to the store. Need to clean out the basement. I tap my fingers on the countertop, trying to get some momentum. But first, I think as I notice again the white band of flesh around my finger, I need to get my damn ring back from little Miss Seven.

Jane

"So what kind of wood is that? It smells like red maple." Her dad furrows his bushy eyebrows

Mike furrows his even bushier brows, his nose sniffing the air like, *not* like a dog. Nothing dog-like about him, Jane thinks as she pulls open the screen door to stand outside in the cold March air with Mike and her dad. More like a raccoon, a wild creature nesting on the borders of civilization. His nostrils alive to the night, little black hairs visible, tickled with scent.

"Maple? Out here?" Mike looks around, as if a forgotten woodpile will materialize in his front yard.

"No, in your Franklin stove." Her dad gestures toward the little puffs of smoke flowing out of the Silverstein's trim white colonial house. They are all three standing outside the door to Mike's house now, Jane, Dad, and Mike, who's shivering in the cold night air.

"Oh. I don't know. Yeah, maybe it's maple. Shoshanna takes care of that. Gets it from some guy down at the nurseries at Cornell."

"It smells like maple. It will clog your flue," her dad proclaims with certainty. "The sap congeals when the temperature hits above a hundred or so degrees. Pine is what you want. The Cornell Nursery guy can get you some. It'll cost you a bit more, ten bucks per cord, but it'll save you a lot of grief. The flue is a bitch to clean once the sap has gummed it all up." A goofy smile flickers across Mr. Schwartz's face for a second, as if it can't decide where to land.

She watches as Mike lets the smile perch across his own lips. He nods agreeably. Her cheeks burn as her father talks on and on.

"So Jane is doing okay with her Hebrew?"

"Oh yeah. Her Hebrew was pretty good to start."

The goofy smile has traveled back to Mr. Schwartz. He squints a little, nostrils still sniffing. "I figure that's the most important part. Learning the Hebrew. Trains your brain to decode symbols. That comes in handy in chemistry."

"And in synagogue." Mike smiles hard to indicate that this is a joke. Mr. Schwartz barks out a laugh. It's a 'heh heh heh' laugh, the h's aspirated hard, like in a comic book character's laugh. Just SHUT UP, Jane thinks silently, trying to aim her thoughts like a missile precisely at her father's laughter. She feels a trickle of wet winding down her leg. Will she bleed onto the white concrete steps? Leave bloody tracks down Mike's driveway as she walks to her dad's car? Drown in blood before they get home?

"Dad, I gotta go to the bathroom."

"Well, hurry it up. I'll be waiting in the car." Her father nods a good-bye to Mike, and abruptly turns away, walking down the porch stairs to his car.

In Mike's bathroom, the tiled walls are white. The tub and sink are whiter, bone-pale, like endless blank sheets of paper. Lipsticks, organic soaps, bottles of honey-lemon shampoo for curly hair, more soaps. Soap enough for a hygienic family of ten, and lipsticks, an embarrassment of lipsticks, enough for a whole army of well-dressed women, jumble together on a smooth white countertop. Eight toothbrushes rest against one another in a little white plastic cup near the sink, their brush-heads conspiratorially bent over. Why would two people need eight toothbrushes? Do they have company a lot? Or just like to use different brushes on different days? Is there a special Shabbos toothbrush, a High Holy Days tooth brush? A mikvah toothbrush for Shoshanna?

Jane has never considered whether Shoshanna uses the mikvah or not. But now in the presence of her oatmeal soaps, her multiple toothbrushes, her sanitary napkins "for heavy flow days" in a jumbo-sized box stashed behind the toilet, now Jane wonders. Does she go to the mikvah? She's a law school student, not an Orthodox housewife. It's hard to imagine Shoshanna submerged in the mikvah waters, naked to God. Preparing beforehand, standing in front of this very mirror, examining her body from top to bottom. Jane thinks of Shoshanna in motion, her pearl earrings glinting in the light as she hurries down the Silverstein's driveway to her car, her tailored pants suits flashing orange, peach, lemon as she runs off to her late-night constitutional law study group. "I love constitutional, but it's the toughest," she told Jane once, conspiratorially winking as she hurried out the door. Does she love mikvah? Remove her pearls, eye shadow, jangly bracelets, strip down and cleanse for Mike?

She'd have to go to Binghamton, a good two-hour drive

in the snow, to find a synagogue Orthodox enough to have a mikvah. Jane's already done the research. Binghamton, Syracuse, and Albany all have them. But surprisingly, Rochester, with its big Conservative temple, its new Jewish Community Center, its dentists and doctors from the expanded Medical Center, has none. The secretary at the Center had laughed when she realized what Jane was asking for; even over the phone, her embarrassment had traveled. "Oh no, dear. We don't have anything like that. We're not Orthodox, you know."

A window above the sink is cracked open. Cold air and the scent of burning wood drafts in to the bathroom. Is it maple she smells, this heavy, resiny scent? It'll clog up Mike's flue. She imagines the bathroom on fire, the white walls curling up in flames, everything white and red and hot. And a red maple leaf suspended in the center of the flames, unmarred by fire, like the burning bush in the Bible. She can't remember who it was who saw the burning bush. Mike would know.

She can hear the grumble of her father's car in the driveway. Time to go home for dinner, maybe spaghetti topped with broccoli, or chicken with green beans, or cold cuts and asparagus spears. Her mother has a green vegetable for every dish. However junky the rest of the meal may be, there is always one good green vegetable. Lima beans and franks. Spinach and steak. Jane grabs a lime green soap that she expects to smell minty, but it's unscented. And pockets it in her lime green ski jacket as she closes the door.

In the car, she sucks on her hair and examines her fingers. She imagines Mrs. Walkeson scrutinizing her cuticles, clicking her tongue in mock-disgust as she pushes the ragged flesh back.

CHAPTER 8:
MONDAY

Jane

Outside Jane's window, clouds hang in grey heavy puffs, like smoke blown from an old man's pipe. Three of them group together, puff puff puff. Lying on her back in her bed, Jane can stare straight up into the sky. The window is half-covered by yellow curtains, allowing light to glare into the room. Her fingers circle around her nipples. They swell up to meet her, the left one a little larger than the right as she looks out at the sky. Each cloud should have a name: Leah One, Old Leah, and Leah Junior. You're my number one Leah, she tells Leah One, who is the fairest of them all, with only a little smudge of grey darkening her corner. Jane pinches her right nipple to make it even with the left, holding her pinky out as she pinches as if she were an English princess sipping a cup of tea.

Is it swelling? Is it still smaller than the other? She pulls at it, rubs it with her forefinger until it hardens. There: now both nipples are the same size. She exhales, relieved.

Leah, smallish Leah. Get your tits ready for me.

If she squints, the clouds blur together, one Leah meshing with another, grey white black. A matrix of Leahs, Leah Leah Leah. Leah, who spelled backwards is still almost Leah.

Ha-el.

Leah. Jane visualizes the letters in bright orange, adds neon lights edging around the borders, diamond studs to their surface. Anything to drown out dumb old God.

Go build the damn mikvah, Leah my girlie. Go.

The voice is getting louder, and talking faster, like a series of quick light bullets battering her skull.

But God, right now I have my period. Isn't the whole point of the mikvah to purify women from their, you know, menses?

Leah! You're wasting my time. Didn't you read Rabbi Akiba? In Rabbi Loewe's *Jewish Path in Sex, Love, and Marriage*?

I thought I did, Jane stutters in a whisper. I thought he was very clear on the need to be clean before entering the mikvah.

Page 53, God hisses. Read page 53, and then even you will understand.

She gets off the bed and pulls her shirt back down, humming in time to the voice.

From under her pillow she pulls out Rabbi Loewe, flipping so fast to page 53 that she accidentally rips page 32. Damn.

But page 32 is maybe the whole point. *Mikvah: Exclusions and Exceptions.* — *Female*, reads the section header at the top of the page. She reads each word carefully:

"The mikvah, contrary to popular belief, does not promote shame about the female body. It glories in it! The exceptions to the rules of t'annit niddeh demonstrate this clearly. Rabbi Akiba suggests the onset of menses are to be celebrated, for now a marriage can be performed, a mikvah can be entered, the order of the world, the purity of the race upheld by the woman's monthly cycles."

So she can go! The thrill of it charges through her, counterpoint to the cramps: *I can go to the mikvah now.* Technically, a girl is not to go until her wedding night, but exceptions are made in those rare cases, Rabbi Loewe carefully reminds his readers, when a woman is to perform a ritual function outside of her normal duties of candle-lighting and child-bearing. And the clincher: *Exceptions are made and one may enter the mikvah at otherwise prohibited times (such as in the middle of menstruation) when the benefits of performing the mikvah ritual would outweigh the violation to the law.*

"So you were right, God," she calls out loud, her words sounding strange and loud in the empty room. But he doesn't answer. God's voice has fallen silent. Jane holds the page in her lap, waiting for another page to fall out of the book, another sign from God to appear.

Out the window, she can see the clouds are darkening, preparing for a storm. Across the way, the Walkeson's house is lit up , the windows sparkling with light like candles on a birthday cake. Mrs. Walkeson must be home at least, if not awake. Without bothering to grab a coat, Jane races down the stairs, out the front door, onto the monorail, across to the Walkeson's kitchen door.

The screen door is open, the kitchen lights all ablaze as if they've been waiting for her footsteps. The door swings open easily. "Mrs. Walkeson? Are you up? It's Jane from next door."

A purple fluorescent, planted above an out-of-season hibiscus plant in the living room, buzzes asthmatically.

"Mrs. Walkeson?"

A white figure appears in the doorway. Mrs. Walkeson, in

a white bathrobe, with a white towel on her head, like a heron, a fine-boned bird. Mrs. Walkeson, pausing before flight. Jane has never her seen her without a wig before, she realizes. She cuts a more solid figure wigless, more substantial, all angles and edges.

"Jane! I wasn't expecting you. Are you sick again?"

Jane shifts her weight, twirling a piece of bang-hair around her tongue. Stupid, you're so stupid, she reprimands herself silently as she chomps down on it. Of course Mrs. Walkeson doesn't remember about the mikvah. She probably didn't even mean it when she said she'd do it. "No. I just... wanted some help with a research project. I thought you might be able to help."

"Well, I just finished taking my bath, and was about to do a pedicure. Let's do the pedicure first, and then I'll see if I can help you out."

Jane nods vigorously, her mouth filled with hair.

"So Jane, maybe you can help me with my pedicure. It's so much easier having someone else do it, don't you think? I can never do my right foot properly." She smiles, her large white teeth glinting like well-manicured pale toes.

"No problem, Mrs. Walkeson. What colors do you like?"

"Oh, pinks, purples. Anything in a frost. Not red, though. Too trampy."

Jane laughs, following Mrs. Walkeson into the bathroom. She kneels on the floor in front of the closed toilet seat, as if Mrs. Walkeson is already perched on the seat, legs dangling down, toes waiting for their lacquer bonnets.

But Mrs. Walkeson stands. By the window, the funny shaped oval window with the thick glass pane and the ledge against which Mrs. Walkeson leans her elbows. Jane can see

Mrs. Walkeson's bones sticking out of the thin nightgown meeting on the ledge, the upper and lower arm bones stabbing into the ledge. She's gotten thinner, wispier, like an unfinished figure drawing, the outlines of bones and muscles more visible than the person.

Jane organizes the nail polishes in a purple-and-pink rainbow, by intensity of shade rather than color. Darker colors to her left, lights to her right. Mrs. Walkeson sighs. Jane has to pee. She watches the toilet seat, white and motionless, silently hoping Mrs. Walkeson will sit so they can get on with the pedicure and Jane can then pee.

She doesn't sit down. Jane takes out Midnight Plum Scandal and paints her left pinkie and her thumb nails. As she bends over to finish up the thumb nail, a piece of her hair catches on the painted surface, making the polish all bumpy and messy. "Damn!" she yells too loud, trying to lick off the polish from the ends of her hair and repaint the messed-up thumb nail at the same time.

"So how exactly does this bath thing work?" Mrs. Walkeson asks, looking far out into the oval window, not turning to face Jane.

"Your bath?" Jane is choking a little on the combination of hair and nail polish, a clot forming in her throat like a wooden fist. Now swallow. Don't choke. Don't puke.

"No no. You know, that Jewish bath thing. For cancer."

"Oh, you mean mikvah." Keep swallowing, Jane wills her throat as her fingers rearrange the nail polishes, this time by brand name. Revlon. Maybelline. L'Oreal, pronounced Laurie-Elle.

Mrs. Walkeson stretches her long neck to one side, considering this. "Yeah, that's it. Like that one you were

191

trying to rig up in my basement."

Jane takes out the wand of Corvette Cream and does the remaining nails on her hands as the words spill out. "Well, we need two sources of water: one running, one still. That's why I wanted to use the sauna and kiddie pool; we can run a hose in there pretty easily for the running water. I tried using the inner tube for the still water, but it didn't work. I think it will be okay with if we just fill the kiddy pool and have that be the, you know, symbolic still water. We fill it up, we run the hose in, and then we take a bath beforehand. Oh—and we have to remove everything. I mean *everything*: makeup, jewelry, deodorant. And then we dunk three times, and then it's over!"

Mrs. Walkeson turns around and sits on the toilet seat, extending her bare feet out before Jane. She wiggles her toes a little. "Is there anything you haven't thought of, missy? Well, I guess I'm game. As long as we don't mess up Mr. Walkeson's sauna too much, I think it's okay. What would Susie think?!"

Jane laughs. "We can turn the sauna on afterwards, to dry things up. They'll never know!"

"So is there anything else I should know about mikvah? Like how it cures cancer?"

Jane bites her lip. For once she can't tolerate the thought of hair in her throat, hair in her mouth, hair tickling against her lip. Instead she shakes the lightest of the nail polishes, Peach Frost Surprise, and opens the bathroom vanity, where she knows from past inspections the cotton balls are ensconced. Between her legs the thick pad shifts, scraping against her inner thigh. "Well, there are some other rules about it, but they're not really followed anymore. It works to clean things out, wash out all the impurities and stuff."

"Well, I sure have lots of impurities and stuff in me! So do you think God will care if we have painted toenails in the mikvah? From the way this polish stinks, I think the chemicals in it will help the mikvah kill off all the impurities."

Puffy and round, wisping at the edges like the Leah clouds, the cotton balls cling to each other in the bag. Jane separates one and pops it between Mrs. Walkeson's big right toe and the one beside it. Is it called an index toe? "I think nail polish is okay. As long as it doesn't flake off or anything under water. So we should probably use a top coat."

"Clear works okay for that. There should be some near where you got the cotton balls."

Mrs. Walkeson starts to hum as Jane gets the clear polish out from under the sink. Michelle, my bell. Hum de hum de hum. These words, understand, my Michelle.

"Michelle, my bell, You had better go, straight to hell, my Michelle," Jane sings loudly, punching out the words as she lacquers on the clear polish. Mrs. Walkeson doesn't laugh; she just keeps humming, adding a "Michelle, my bell" every few hums.

"So which color do you want for the mikvah? White is purity. So whatever's closest to white is best, I guess."

"Do you think fuchsia would work?" Mrs. Walkeson picks Fuchsia Frosted Fantasy up carefully, as if it might explode. A nail bomb, fuchsia frosting the windows, floor, toilet seat. Who would be liable? Would the owner of the polish still be liable if the polish itself were part of the preparations for the mikvah, a pure and holy pursuit? Would intent outweigh its outcome? Surely there is a Talmudic example close enough to be applied to the case of exploding polish. Mrs. Walkeson's humming has switched to the later Beatles, "Dear Prudence, won't you come out to plaaaaahey?"

"Yeah, fuchsia's okay. You can do mine fuchsia, too." Jane carefully places one cotton ball between each of Mrs. Walkeson's toes. How does Mrs. Walkeson keep her nails so clean? As she polishes, she hums along with "Dear Prudence," filling in the missing lyrics Mrs. Walkeson hums through.

Fuchsia for mikvah. Jane imagines them together in the mikvah, only their fuchsia toes glowing in the darkness.

Charlene

"Okay, we're ready! It's mikvah time."

Jane likes being in charge. Our toenails are barely dry, and already she's commandeering us down into the mikvah. "Now you have to remove EVERYTHING. I guess we can wait 'til we get to the dunking part to take off our clothes, but we should strip off everything else up here." I take off my ring and earrings. Jane squints her eyes over my face, scanning each inch for contamination. "Um, I think the wig has to go, too."

I pull it off in one motion, grabbing the top by the roots. It's a red bouffant, shoulder-length number, with thick bangs in front. I throw it into the garbage can by the bathroom sink. It feels good to be rid of it. No more wigs, I think as it makes a satisfying, puffy noise as it hits the can. Only skin and bones and mikvah. My new formula.

"Oh— and we need to shower before the mikvah. You see, the mikvah's not a real bath; it's just symbolic. You're supposed to scrub really hard, in every place you can think of, and make sure you rinse all the soap off." She hands me a bar of soap. "I'll wait outside."

In the shower, I manipulate the soap between my thighs, under my arms, on the soles of my feet, between my toes. Where else? I scrub beneath my nails, beneath my toenails, in my ass crack. The water is too hot, turning my skin a violet red. I don't make it cooler. The purple polish on my toenails blends in with reds of my skin, like a layer of dark sediment covering the topsoil. "This is much better than licorice hot chocolate," I call out to Jane, who surely can't hear me.

While Jane takes her shower, I check for any remaining dirt on my body, as Jane has instructed. I swivel the wax out of my ears with a Q-tip. I Q-tip inside my belly button. I wipe my vagina with a paper towel, the super-absorbent kind. What else is left to clean?

Jane comes out with a towel on her head, queen of clean. "Okay, I think we're ready." I notice a little bit of rose-colored lipstick smudging beyond the boundaries of her lips. I guess the mikvah rules don't prohibit her from stealing my lipstick. She is regal, her strong features accented by the towel-turban like a small princess, a miniaturized version of an actual queen.

I take a towel from the rack beside the sauna, a threadbare violet one that I've let Bill keep down here from our old house in Washington, and turban my bald head with it to match Jane's. "Now we're ready. Lead on, mikvah missy!"

Our basement is really a mess. Will anyone clean it up after I'm gone? Or will this mess outlive me? The Chubby Checker records Bill kept from college molding in the corner—will they survive longer than me? The broken two-wheeler Mary abandoned when she got married, my old accounting books from college, filled with notes and numbers scribbled in my hand—is it worse to think of them outliving me, or to think of someone else cleaning them out after I'm dead?

I'm only allowing myself this corny kind of thinking because of the mikvah, the sneaky hope of cure rooting itself in the very word as it forms on my tongue. Mikvah. I wonder if Jane has made it up, if there's really any such a thing. How would she even know about it? Her family certainly doesn't seem religious; they don't keep kosher or anything, though they don't have a Christmas tree or Santa Claus decorations, either, during the holiday season.

"Where's the light?" Jane calls, her voice ringing in the darkness.

"Here." She may run the mikvah, but in my basement, I run the lights. Basements never do get fully lit; no matter how strong the bulbs overhead are, no amount of watts can mimic the sun down here. I like that about the basement. I like it better than the natural light in these parts, anyway. Here in Ithaca, the light is always either a bright glare or a foggy haze. But down here, it's yellow and intense. The dark eats up the space as you move away from the 120-watt bulb hanging in the middle of the ceiling from some fishing wire.

"So why don't you say a little prayer or something and I'll set it up." Jane is hesitant now, not the commanding mikvah leader she was in the bathroom.

"Okay. But the only prayer I still know by heart is the Lord's Prayer."

"I think that's okay. I don't know the right prayer for the

mikvah, and anything is better than nothing."

"Our father who art in heaven, hallowed be thy name, 'til kingdom come thy will be done, in earth as it is in heaven." The words tumble out from some dusty old Methodist tape lodged in my brain.

"That's pretty," Jane remarks as she unwinds the hose.

"That's not the whole thing. There's more: give us this day, our—"

"Wait—where's the light to the sauna?"

The sauna. I've forgotten about the sauna, our designated mikvah site. There it sits in the middle of the basement, freestanding, like a portable toilet at a ball game. It's a piss-ugly green that looks dark and mossy in this light. It's Bill's, not mine really.

Bill loves mail-order gadgets. First there was the electric can opener, a clunky white plastic number with a hideous daisy-infested plastic cover. Then came Mr. Coffee and his wife, Mrs. Tea. Then electric shavers, his and hers. He likes matching sets, boy and girl appliances. After we moved out here to Hunters Lane, the gadgets got bigger, bulkier, pricier. The foot massager. The electric food cart. The orange juicer. And then finally the sauna.

"Okay, you blow up the pool while I mop the floor of the sauna. Everything has to be spotless for a proper mikvah." Somehow, she has found a bucket and pail. We're no longer on prayers; it's all practicalities now. The Lord's Prayer and whatever else I can dredge up will have to wait.

"But Jane, how are you going to fit the pool inside the sauna, er, mikvah door once it's blown up?"

She stares at me with a grimace, as if this technicality is my fault. Please don't cry, I think, even though she looks more angry than sad. My brain clicks into action: a plan, make a plan.

"I know," I say too brightly. "I'll help you mop, and then we'll blow it up inside." She nods, the grimace dissolving, and disappears into the netherlands of the basement.

A rag appears from the same mysterious source as the bucket and pail. "Now really scrub," she commands, her turban knocked a bit off-center. There is something elegant about the sauna, I have to admit. It's like a spaceship from a low-budget T.V. movie. The walls are that odd plastic green, and everything inside looks smooth and flat. Two foldout benches tucked into the wall. There's a little window on one side, out of which we have a scenic view of two old tricycles leaning against one another like lovers. We leave the benches up without discussing it. The floor is really dirty—that thick, moldy sort of grime is growing all over, turning the ground a licheny light green.

"Do you want the light on?" I ask. The bulb in the center of the basement throws a few rays into the sauna, turning our skin a sepia color. We could be in a silent movie, with the legend MAKING THE MIKVAH appearing in white lettering beneath us.

"No. I like it like this."

"Um, Jane? I think we'd better shower again once the floor is cleaned up. I'm getting pretty grimy."

She looks up at me, hair frizzing out of the back of the turban towel. On her hands and knees, her head tilting up to talk to me, she looks like a wild animal pausing to consider its prey, the hair and turban haloing like a mane around her. "Or we could just hose down here." Her eyes are squinting as she talks.

"But then the whole basement will get wet. Mr. Walkeson won't like that at all! And judging from the bottom of the sauna, there's already enough moisture down here to grow an army of bacteria."

"Yeah, but I figured out where the drain is in the basement floor. I guess it's to prevent flooding. So the water won't really collect. I mean, we'll have to get rid of the mikvah water, too, after we're done. So either way, things will get a little wet." Even on her hands and knees, she looks regal, a princess of the basement waterways.

"Okay."

And on goes the hose, blasting my towel turban, soaking my maroon blouse and slacks. "Jane, we should do this OUTSIDE the sauna."

"Okay," she says reluctantly, hose in hand. She pushes open the door, and gestures for me to go out first. I feel the water spray my butt as I step out into the basement. She's not going to leave the sauna now: this I know. With one hand on her hip and one hand training the hose onto me, she sprays me down.

It's cold. I've forgotten how cold water can be. Hot and cold water: two different birds entirely. Jane is neither sadistic nor gentle with the hose. She stands matter-of-factly in front of me, carefully aiming it at every part of my body. Her eyes are trained on mine, never flickering down to take in the rest of body. Naked, I feel lighter, more confident, the dank air of the basement enveloping me. I do a little jig in a circle, so I get clean all over.

"Now you," I command, grabbing the hose from Jane's hand. I put a finger on the spigot so that it will be more like a shower. She's taken off her towel turban and shoes. Barefoot, in a red t-shirt and blue jeans, standing in the door of my husband's sauna, she turns her back to me and strips.

She stays turned away, the bones of her back peeking through her skin. I can see the string of a tampon hanging out between her legs, dangling like a white worm. So that's it.

I spray carefully: neck, head, back, legs, butt. Her hair absorbs the water. It hangs like a satin curtain, thick and shiny, the curls straightening out, uncoiling.

And then we are ready to inflate.

"My lungs are bigger, so I'll start." I put my mouth on the lip of the inner tube. Usually, I let Susie do it herself. It's a cheap kiddie pool, bought as an afterthought at Jamesway's on a hot July, three or four years ago, back when Mary was still with Rick, and Susie was still at the age where a blue plastic pool could provide instant happiness. "Grandma's pool," she called it, giving me a little flirtatious smile as she tried to blow it up.

Now Jane is getting restless with nothing to do. "Let me do it," she says after I've blown it almost to the end. Grabbing it out of my hands, she inhales a big, theatrical breath before she blows. Her cheeks puff up, pink and full, like overblown balloons. "You wait outside," she gasps,

I stand right outside the sauna, almost in the doorway, watching. She is fully in charge now, finishing it up, careful not to let the air escape as she plugs the pool up. Her stomach is bloated slightly, pressing out against the blue plastic. Does she have cramps? Did she tell her mother yet? Has she gotten it before?

"Okay," she calls to me, "Now we've got to fill it with water. I was going to get a second water source in here somehow, but I think there's only room enough for the hose. So pass it to me." I pass it to her, as she's commanded. The pool can only take about a foot or so of water; otherwise, the sides will overflow. Should I remind her? I decide not to. She'll figure it out. And she does: I see her eyeing the fragile blue skin of the pool's side as she aims the hose toward the pool. "Turn it on," she commands, and I do, twisting the green spigot in the little corner sink hidden behind the sauna. Jane sings a little Jewish song to herself as she fills it up. "Baruch atah adonai elohanu meloch ha'olam..."

A foot of water fills the kiddie pool, enough to splash over the sides. The blue body of the pool shivers, saturated by the water, but the structure holds. Don't fill it any more, I telepathically beg Jane. It'll overflow.

And she doesn't. She gestures for me to turn the water off; I do, and then come to stand in the doorway of the sauna. We smile at each other.

To prepare for a mikvah is one thing; to do it is another. The kiddy pool filled, the hose in place, our respective bodies scrubbed to a shine, we hesitate. What now? Is this really too silly? We look at each other.

And then Jane is our fearless leader again. "Okay, it's ready. I'll close my eyes while you get in the mikvah. There's only about a foot of water here, so you'll have to kneel down in it, and then I'll help you dunk three times." She covers her eyes with her left hand, kneeling in the water to demonstrate. "Geez it's cold! I'm getting goose bumps."

"Should I say a prayer or something?" I ask.

"We can say the regular 'barucha'; it's kind of a catch-all prayer. I'll say each word as you get ready, and you can repeat after me."

"Baruch"

"Baruch"

"Atah"

"Atah"

Why did we decide to make a mikvah? Out of the sauna's window, I spy Mary's old aquarium. It's just an empty glass bowl now. Why, oh why on earth are we making a mikvah? Wouldn't an aquarium be a better bet?

"Elohanu meloch ha'olum"

"Elohanu meloch ha'olum" Jane is peeking out at me from between her fingers, staring directly at my breasts, my appendix scar, my hairy crotch. I step into the sauna. There's hardly any room to stand; the mikvah-kiddy pool takes up all the space. It seems like there's no oxygen, either: only the blue of the bath and the white of Jane's skin.

"Asher kideshanu b'mitvotav"

She's getting nervous, eager to get on with it.

"Asher kideshanu b'mitzvotav"

"Vitvivanuh lihadleeknair"

"You have to repeat that one, Jane." I stare at the eye that is peeking out at me. She covers it again.

"Let's just get to the end: shell mikvah."

"Shell mikvah!" And I step into the mikvah.

It's freezing. An icicle bath. The cold of the water stings, as if my body is covered in open wounds and I'm in a tub of rubbing alcohol. The goose bumps cover my skin like fancy wallpaper. Jane giggles as I splash around, crouching down to my knees. I hunch my shoulders a bit so that my breasts are covered by the water. "So now what?"

"Okay. You have to be totally submerged. Only total immersion counts; otherwise it doesn't work. Three immersions, and you're set. So lean back three times, and I'll yell 'kosher' each time so God hears that you've done it." She is kneeling on her knees, too, so that the water comes up to her neck. I notice again the little white string peeping out between her legs. So she's started her menses. I half-remember something she'd said when we'd talked about mikvah the other day, when I caught her skulking around in my basement. Something about mikvah and menstruation. What was it? You're supposed to do the mikvah before, or after you get your period? I shake my head, the memory not quite forming. I clench my fists, trying to keep the cold from freezing up my extremities.

I want my ring back. The pale ring of skin around my finger looks red under water, like a burn. I've got to get my ring back from her. Don't forget this time!

"Starting now?"

She nods, lips blue with cold. She is facing me, ready for the count. The pink polish on her nails glistens like frosted bubble gum as she grabs my shoulders and pushes me back. The water meets me and I am under.

I remember back dives like this. As a girl I'd arch back effortlessly off the dock, springing up and back and down, the water climbing up to take me.

The water takes me.

Leah, daughter of God, sister of Rachel, sister of Jane, swim under.

The water is humming, alive with sound, a voice, not a voice, pure voice singing water across and through her.

In the beginning was water. And then...

Just as the voice starts to tell me the story of the origins of water, I surface.

"Kosher!" Jane's voice rings out as I gasp for air. "Wow! You were under for, like, a whole minute!"

As the oxygen hits my lungs and I straighten up onto my knees and Jane's voice chirps out everything blurs a moment. And swirls into focus.

"I need my ring back, Jane."

"Shh! You're supposed to do it three times without stopping. Go back under!"

And her hands push my shoulders back again.

The water softens my bones. Like eels they bend and sway inside my body, the calcified infrastructure twisting, the marrow inside melting into water. Flesh? No flesh. No meat. No thickening arteries, lumpy fat, stringy tendons. No lymphy nodes and knobs. Only bones, softened back to their uterine malleability.

I lean back, arching until the water rushes over my head and its bones, too, are softened. That strange underwater sound, tuneless, all notes no notes voice swelling in my ears as the water pours over me.

Leah, Leah. A strange hand is caressing my head, whispering in my ears as they fill with water. Even though the hand is out of my field of vision, stroking the back of my head, the curve where the head turns to neck, I can see it. Ringless, slender, long fingers with short nails polished a pearly white stroke each pore on my scalp, massaging deep into the ghost roots, the unseen follicles. In the beginning was water.

"And then what?" I mouth to the hand.

And I'm breaking through the surface again.

"What?" I croak aloud, with Jane yelling "Kosher" only inches from my ear. "Kosher!" she yells again, as if I hadn't heard. The blue of the kiddie pool glows in the dim light. What a phony color.

I lean back down before she can push me. Waterlogged: that's what this is. Mild hallucinations due to oversaturation. I lean farther back, feeling gravity embrace me, dance me to the blue floor of the mikvah.

This time the hand is invisible, but I feel it massaging my scalp again. I resist surfacing this time, my arms reaching out to the sides of the kiddie pool to keep myself underwater. I am all lungs, swallowing water in chokes and sputters as my unwilling head pushing up into the air.

"Kosher!"

And it's over.

We are clasping hands, bouncing up and down, splashing water, giggling and giggling. All modesty has vanished. We face each other and jump as high as we can, synchronized, perfect. Woop! Up go my breasts as I jump.

I feel something slip onto my finger. The ring, glinting against my waterpuckered skin, hugging my finger. How did she slip it on with our hands clasped so tight? What a sneak. I smile at Jane, and she blushes.

We stop jumping, our hands still clasped.

"Congratulations, Mrs. W.! You are officially purified from disease, decay, and dirt. Do you feel any different? Cleaner or anything?"

I take stock. "I feel....like I could breathe under water. Like I don't need oxygen. Not cleaner, exactly; more like—I don't know, it's hard to explain. Like the boundaries are blurred. Like when you run in a circle, and then stop and watch the earth tilt back and forth."

Jane is deciding whether this is kosher. "Do you think it

helped the cancer?"

I laugh, unclasping my fingers from hers. I stand up in the pool. Naked and cold, teeth chattering, I cross my arms over my breasts to cover the nipples. "I don't know. Too soon to tell, I guess. It did feel like there was some sort of...presence. Not God exactly, but something. Like the water wanted to help me out."

Jane stands up, swinging her legs over the side of the pool, and stands shivering in the little space left in the sauna. I see a flash of dark burgundy on her inner thigh. Should I say something about it? "Did we forget to bring towels down here?" she says, looking around, turning her back to me so I can't see her thighs or breasts or period.

"Yeah. Listen, I'll go up and get them. Why don't you start cleaning up? You can drag the pool out and pour the water straight down the basement drain. I'll bring a mop, too, so we can clean up all the water we've splashed on the floor."

In the upstairs bathroom, I sit at my window a minute, taking stock of my naked body. Outside the air is thick, grey, spring temporarily called off in favor of late winter. I lean on the window ledge, tracing around the circumference of the hexagonal window-frame with my index finger.

EPILOGUE:
MONDAY, ONE WEEK LATER

Charlene

It was on the seventh day that I felt it. I awakened late that morning, groggy from a long night. We had made love well past midnight, tearing into each other too hard, unthinking, ripping into each other's skin, buttocks, mouths, more. "Are you okay?" Bill asked afterwards, touching my ribcage tentatively, as if to check for broken bones. "I'm okay," I repeated. I flipped away from him, onto my side. But my skin felt strange, alive, as if the blood vessels were about to burst through the surface.

Everything was overripe in the morning: my thighs thick and sticky, the sheets stinking damp, tightly wrapped around my sweaty body. The sun broke early, a thick bright yoke sliding across the sky, the sort that sticks to the pan, difficult to clean up. My face was greasy to the touch, slick with oil. My skin no longer tingled. Need to get up. Need to clean this house, my skin, the basement. Need to call Dr. S. for more pills. I twisted the sheets off and stood.

It wasn't until after showering that I peered in the mirror and saw it. At first I thought it was an effect of the humidity, the moist air leaving the glass partly clouded, partly clear. Above my head, close to the crown, was a blurry red penumbra.

I rubbed the surface of the mirror, feeling its hard, flat surface. It's just glass, really, I thought. How odd that we know our own visages only through glass. The mirror smudged a bit under the oily pressure of my fingertips, but the red area remained clouded.

A slipped halo, I thought, stitched tight to my skull instead of suspended above. Dust particles, arranged around my head in a circle, suspended by some electromagnetic force emanating from my brain. Or an effect of heat, an optical illusion. A mirage, like the pools of water seen dripping across the pavement on long summer drives.

Hair was the last possibility to enter my mind. For it was still the bald lady, brown eyes glaring out, cheekbones angled sharp and chiseled, skull smooth and bare, who stared back at me. Humpty Dumpty's oldest daughter: a familiar reflection by now, this pale hairless creature, more familiar somehow than the orange, yellow, black, brown-wigged lady I'd glimpse throughout my day in window glasses, the eyes of strangers, this very mirror. Mirrors really shouldn't be trusted, anyway. Glass, smooth dumb glass, our only source of reflection, I mused as I scratched my head and stared at the red smudge.

Hair. Only bristly peach fuzz, to be sure, but hair nonetheless. I fingered my whole head in shock, feeling the sharp bristles scratch against my fingers. I moved closer to the mirror.

Hair. Not just any hair, but bright carroty orange hair, sprouting all over my head. Red hair, growing from my scalp.

Hair.

I ran my fingers through it, mesmerized. There wasn't

much of it, but it was glorious. Soft to the touch, the fuzz crowned my head.

Whose hair was this?

The color certainly wasn't mine. Even when I was in college and had a brief flirtation with peroxide, I'd never done it red. Sure, I had red wigs, but they were Technicolor, so far removed from anything found in nature that it might as well have been blue. My own brown mouse hadn't even had hints of auburn in it; its muddy light sienna lent itself more easily to blonde than to red. And this red bore no similarity to auburn, was not even a second cousin to brown. True red, as vivid and natural a red as I've ever seen sprouting out of a head.

It's Jane's, I thought for a strange long moment, even though I knew full well that Jane's hair is brown, not red.

And then I made myself a cup of tea, settled down with the t.v. on the gold couch, and fell into a long, dreamless sleep.

Jane

In the beginning there was water.

Oceans uninterrupted by land, a world of fish and coral, a blue green globe of water, spinning around the sun. Inside the globe, at its very center, slept God, covered in scales and gills. Since there were no men to disturb him, no women to worry after, mostly he slept, bubbles from his snores traveling up to the surface of the great uninterrupted ocean.

Occasionally he would go for a swim, doing backstrokes and sidestrokes among the schools of lemon-colored fish who lived in the depths alongside him. But mostly, he just slept, covered in scales and gills, bubbling out his snores. Life was peaceful on the water planet, if uneventful.

Oh, there were other Gods, the Air God above, the Sun God even higher, and the sleepy Moon Goddess higher still, but God didn't know about them, for he had no reason to go beyond the surface of the ocean. He mostly stayed at the very bottom of the ocean, like a ship full of sunken treasures. It was warmer in the depths, and the fish were more refined.

One day, God woke from a long, dreamless nap. He felt a bit waterlogged, so he thought he'd go for a nice swim. He caught up with a school of his favorite lemon-colored fish. He was swimming along nicely when he felt something quiver against his scaly chest. "Ugh!" He cried. "What the hell is that?" A fish was caught against his chest, a tiny lemon-colored fish. But on what exactly was the fish caught? He looked more closely, and saw that a lock of thick, bushy black hair was sprouting between the scales of his chest.

"Gross!" He cried, and flung the fish off him, pulling the lock of hair out by the root in the process. The fish, startled by this turn of events, started swimming furiously, still tangled up in the hair. He swam and swam, the hair gathering seaweed, sand, silt, dead fish, and other debris along the way. He swam and swam, the clump of hair gathering more and more junk, until it was big enough to be an island. The little fish slithered out of the muddy lock, and found himself on dry land, standing up on two feet. "Damn!" cried God when he saw the land from his nest below the ocean's surface. And the fish was then called a "damn" forever after. Adam.

Adam, Adam, oh damn, Jane repeats as she opens the stale Oreos carefully. On top of Hunt Hill, the soil is alive with worms, beetles, daddy longlegs, termites. Spring is coming; preparations must be made.

Inside Jane's fortress, a sandy anthill is forming beside her stash of dried goods, a mound of fine dirt with a steady stream of ant commanders directing traffic in and out. Just one Oreo could crush the whole thing, destroy their civilization, submerge the ants in a world of white fluff. She holds a cookie over the hill, watching the ants react to the shadow, running helter skelter, and throws it into the woods for a deer to lunch on later.

A bit of the white Oreo gunk has caught on the end of her hair. Automatically, Jane pulls the lock toward her mouth. The mixture of hair and sugar brushes against her lips. She twists the left side of her lips into a half smile like Mike's, and releases the hair, before it even tickles the tip of her tongue. No more sucking, she thinks severely. That's over. Mrs. Walkeson will be proud: Jane will have better hair than Susie now, if she can just keep from sucking.

Brushing off the Oreo goo from the ends of her hair, she starts going through the rest of the supplies, trying to ascertain which have survived the melting groundwaters, and which must be discarded. Her mouth is wet, still expecting a succulent lock of cookie-coated hair. She grabs another cookie, pops it in her mouth, and continues sorting without further ceremony.

Dr. Jennifer Natalya Fink is a professor of English at Georgetown University, a literacy activist, and an all-around hell-raiser. She is the author of two award-winning novels, *Burn* and *V* (both from Suspect Thoughts Press), and is the founder and Gorilla-in-Chief of The Gorilla Press, an organization that promotes youth literacy through bookmaking. Nominated for the Pulitzer, National Jewish Book, and National Book Award, Fink is also the winner of the Dana Award, *Story* Magazine's short fiction award, and twelve other awards. She is the U.S. judge for the Caine Prize for African Literature (known as the "African Booker"), and has published widely on literature, literacy, and hybridity, most notably in the anthology *Performing Hybridity* (Minnesota), which she co-edited with May Joseph.

Breinigsville, PA USA
19 November 2010
249666BV00001B/13/P